A NIGHT WITH CASANOVA

A

NIGHT WITH

CASANOVA

WOLF MANKOWITZ

Illustrated by

JOHN LAWRENCE

SINCLAIR-STEVENSON

First published in Great Britain by
Sinclair-Stevenson Limited
7/8 Kendrick Mews
London SW7 3HG, England

Copyright © 1991 by Imeartas Limited, Dublin

The right of Wolf Mankowitz to be identified as author of
this work has been asserted by him in accordance with the
Copyright, Designs and Patents Act 1988.

British Library Cataloguing in Publication Data
A CIP catalogue record for this book is available from the British Library.
ISBN: 1 85619 079 X

Typeset by Rowland Phototypesetting Limited
Bury St Edmunds, Suffolk
Printed and bound in Great Britain by
Butler and Tanner Limited, Frome and London

'I CANNOT REMEMBER all the places where Jacques Casanova went in his double character of knight-errant and Wandering Jew, but after many years of this existence he began to find the gates of cities, courts, and castles closed to him.

'My nephew, Waldstein, met him at the Venetian ambassador's and took a great liking to him. Waldstein pretended to believe in magic, and to practise it; he began to talk about the clavicula of Solomon, and of Agrippa.

'"How strange that you should speak to *me* of these things," cried Casanova; "*O! che bella cosa, cospetto!* – how familiar all these things are to me!"

'"If that is so," said Waldstein, "come to Bohemia with me, I am leaving tomorrow."

'Casanova, who had come to an end of his money, his travels, and his adventures, took Waldstein at his word, and became his librarian. In this quality he passed the last years of his life at the Château of Dux near Teplitz . . .'

Prince de Ligne, *Mémoires et Mélanges historiques et littéraires*, Paris, 1828.

(I)

With wet feet I arrived at the inn

ONCE I had decided to escape from this loath-some *château* of Dux, or *schloss* of Duchkov, the enterprise seemed simple enough, and it was difficult to understand why, having entertained the desire to leave for so long, I had found it so hard to make my final exit. A little after midnight I touched up my *maquillage*, put on my short chestnut *perruque*, and gathered together what small negotiable valuables I had left from the extravagant litter of my years, including my gold patchbox, my gold watch (gift of a Contessa), a neat little dagger, and the best of my swords, though I doubted the likelihood of my engaging in the gallantry of duelling at the age of seventy-two. But a good Toledo blade will always fetch money, and a small neat poniard may be inserted between the ribs of an assailant even by a weakling septua-genarian hand. I had only nine gold ducats of Venice and some small silver, all there was to show of my somewhat irregular promised salary of a thousand florins a year as librarian to His Excel-lency of Waldstein for this past endless decade or so, which money has evaporated like all else. The habit of sleep at night being lost to me, it was in the first hours after midnight that I put on my soft leather riding boots, originally of a delicate shade of amber, and quietly made my way through cold endless stone passages to a small door leading into a courtyard from where steps descended to a gate, which I had earlier unbolted, in the outer wall. And thus I appeared upon the wet stones of the steep path leading to my lord of Waldstein's miserable townlet of Duchkov. Repellent name! Farewell, village of phlegm!

I had not walked with careful precision more than a hundred yards when I became aware that my feet, through three pairs of badly repaired silk stockings, were damp and cold. Before I could essay the world, it seemed I must employ the services of a cobbler, for my boots were designed for comfortable stirrups and a time when I was not required to walk more than the width of a lady's chamber or the length of the carpeted approach to the throne of some mighty and grateful benefactor. With wet feet then I arrived at the inn surmounted with the crests of Waldstein-Wallenstein where the first post-chaise of the day could be expected promptly at six of the clock; for never let it be said that Germanic post-chaises failed to run on time.

The innkeeper, one Stichka, a large distasteful barrel of lard and beer with a monstrous red nose, recognized me at once. 'My Lord Casanova!' he exclaimed. 'What an honour, but so late in the evening! Why, I believe, sir, I haven't seen you for more than a month. Yes, indeed, it was a month and more since I prepared for you that quiet little dinner when the old Italian ladyship was visiting

4

us and sent up the message to you.' He laughed coarsely. 'They will all buy a good dinner for Master Casanova, the shameless old strumpets! But you are alone, sir. You are expecting company, no doubt?' He laughed with lecherous intimacy; an unbearable injustice one must suffer, if one has a certain reputation, is other people's lewd enjoyment of it.

I explained to the distasteful menial briefly that I must leave on the first post-chaise about private business of my Lord Waldstein's and that in no circumstances was the fat-nosed fool to blurt out to anyone that I had been in his noxious sty that morning. He grovelled suitably and assured me gravely that His Lordship's interests were his own, offered me supper, which I declined, requesting only a pot of hot chocolate and some brandy. The so-called brandy they produce here is an infusion of plums and gunpowder, but over the years one may develop a taste for it, and it is sovereign against the damp cold. I also requested him to assist me with the removal of my boots, pointing out that they required the immediate attention of a cobbler.

'Why, bless you, sir!' the fawning publican replied, 'there is a Jew-cobbler of sorts in the kitchen awaiting like yourself the first post-chaise. I will have him see to your honour's boots. He has the tools and such in a leathern bag. I'll take them to him at once, sir.'

As I sat over the cooling gritty chocolate, feeling the small fire of the brandy spreading among my dilapidated vitals, I thought (as I do continuously)

5

of my life. Most of the nights of these past years during which I have been as dead having become librarian to an illiterate noblemen, I have filled with my Memoirs; and though the pages are left behind in that fusty corner where I have lived like a rat among dry tasteless books, I nevertheless carry their memory with me. I have reached on paper only the forty-ninth year of my age, infinitely preferable to the seventy-second, though by common agreement, I still do not, on a good day in a poor light and freshly painted, look more than fifty-five. Nevertheless, I have no doubt that my incomplete life will be published, for there are always publishers for posthumous authors who demand no fees. For my part, if I were to be conjured from the ashes and asked my opinion, I would express the gravest doubts about casting my intimate memories before a common herd of which I know nothing but evil. Why then have I written *in extenso* of petty moments of conquest and victory which do not have the significance now of the inflamed pimple on my backside? My apology for myself is that I have wanted to be busy, and to laugh sometimes, and what else is there for a man of too many years to laugh at other than the long joke of his life? And why should I, who have never denied anyone the least gratification, refuse myself this final one? I shall be dead by the time the first bent lecherous eye lights up squinting through the keyhole at my gallantry; and if the author himself is dead, then what matters it to him whether he has readers or not? He does not benefit by one sequin,

6

one thaler, or one ducat from them, and so he owes them nothing, to the Devil with them, let them please themselves as I have always most assiduously pleased myself and no one else. For the chief business of my life has always been to indulge my senses; I never knew anything of greater importance; and now what embitters my old age is that, having a heart as warm as ever, I have no longer the strength necessary to secure a single day such as those blissful many which I owe to charming and ignorant girls. Age, that cruel incurable disease, compels me to be in good health in spite of my inclinations; if one may call the absence of the ability to catch the pox an indication of good health. Not I; I have always felt myself born for the fair sex, and it has, more often than not, recriprocated my feelings; I have loved it dearly, and have been loved by it as often and as much and in as many various ways as possible, or as some have said, impossible. I freely admit to this weakness for good living for I am very much like the rest of humanity would be, had it the good fortune to have been me.

A waft of grease and stale beer and, 'Surely your honour cares for something to eat?' The innkeeper was leaning over me breathing into my ear as if I were deaf or half-asleep. 'A little breast of chicken, perhaps?'

My stomach rumbled in reply, but it is some time since we have been in complete agreement with one another. 'Bring me some of those dry biscuits I sometimes take with my wine,' I told him.

How a dry biscuit dipped in sour wine epito-
mizes these past years! My teeth now are mostly
false, cunning Devil-forged expensive mouth-
bones which rattle like dice in an empty skull,
instruments of pleasure without feeling. Oh, God
in Heaven, for what did you create old age? Answer
there will be none, no explanation of why this vile
catastrophe has overwhelmed me, my teeth grown
troublesome, my amorous powers waned, and I
become what false teeth and a rusty broken sword
make of a cavalier, librarian to the most generous
and affable prince, Count von Waldstein, in his
castle of Dux in Bohemia, Duchkov in the local
execrable language.

This beneficent Count laughs a great deal,
sometimes, I suspect, at me. If I allow him this
privilege, it is because he is a direct descendant of
the great Wallenstein, and much wealth and the
memory of power cling to him, and without his
invitation to be his librarian, this past endlessly
tedious and impoverished decade might have been
even worse. I was introduced to the jolly Count
through his uncle, my dear old friend and patron,
the Prince de Ligne, who amiably presented me as
'the well-known knight-errant de Seingalt and the
Wandering Jew Casanova', which epithets strike
me as being neither appropriate nor pleasant, but,
in the years of my age, I do not take offence so
easily as I did when young, for the weak are more
tolerant than the strong. Without the good offices
of the Prince and the Count, I would now, perhaps,
be living upon the proceeds of the sale of the

diseased favours of some ageing whore; for such is a common end of those who have spent their lives in the pursuit of erotic adventures, lavishing the wealth of their minds and bodies without reserve upon perfect but perfectly unprofitable pleasures. Yet I cannot deny it. I have always been fond of highly seasoned rich dishes, such as macaroni prepared by a skilful Neapolitan cook; the *olla-podrida* of the Spaniards; the glutinous codfish from Newfoundland; game with a strong flavour; and cheese, the perfect state of which is attained when the tiny animalculae formed from its very essence begin to show signs of life. And women, ah, women! Most delicious and highly seasoned of all rich dishes! I was always prone to lose my headstones over women, but I have never counted the cost, for a sanguine temperament has rendered me very sensible to the attractions of voluptuousness. I was always cheerful and ever ready to pass from one enjoyment to another, the chief business of my life being always to indulge my senses, and, though somewhat hampered in my pursuits in these latter years, I will not renege. True, I have developed a disposition towards melancholy, no doubt in consequence of my incapacity for excess. For I am bound to say that excess of *too little* has ever seemed to me more dangerous than excess of *too much*, which last may cause indigestion and an occasional pox, but the other brings sickness and death. So do not tell me of the virtues of restraint. That man who has the means to be unrestrained and holds back, is a fool, for the time will come when he shall entirely

9

lack the means. So, go to it, everyone, and do not waste time listening to anyone who has the time to reminisce.

These biscuits taste better, I think, soaked in brandy than they do in wine. To be perfectly fair to this miserable country, the brandy does have a certain indescribable character once one is used to it.

Many visitors (provided their visit is sufficiently brief) speak of this Dux as a delightful spot, a charming little town with a dear little market-place filled with respectful little round grubby people and pots and pans and heaps of vegetables, below the great gateways of the monstrous castle (like all Germanic things, enormous and empty, or delightful and little, but always out of proportion to human experience, a dream-castle, but the dream is a nightmare, of which the little people are inordinately proud) constantly pointing out to one another that it is as as any truly royal palace. At the back of it there are great gardens neglected and overgrown as in the midst of the country, pleasant enough if the weather is not either very cold or unbearably hot, which it always is. Then room after room, corridor after corridor, bedecked with gloomy, accusing portraits of that dreary conqueror Wallenstein, and great canvases, poorly painted, of his battles.

But the library (formerly a chaos of volumes) is now, I do not hesitate to claim, one of the best in Europe. The manuscript of the most famous book in Bohemian literature (*Bohemian* literature!), the history of the Church by one Skala, is here, if anyone is ever sufficiently interested to care. And there are more significant and readable volumes (including my own), among the twenty-five thousand which have kept me company for so long, next to a freezing, rusting armoury, with, beyond it, another vast room containing pottery collected quite without selection or taste by the Count on his eastern travels, and then still other rooms full of curious, sometimes obscene, mechanical toys and ivory carvings. Some of the least of those treasures, so carelessly imprisoned, would have purchased me comfortable lodgings in a civilized country for the rest of my life. But the noble Count does not give me presents, and I am too old to steal successfully. Still, what delights me in my old age is independent of the place which I inhabit, for when I am not thinking of the past, I am asleep and dreaming of it, awakening to blacken paper with my memories; which then I read with bitterness at

11

what my pen has vomited up. Which reminds me, the macaroni at supper (an article of my contract with the Count) was as flaccid as an old man's gums. The Count's cook is an excrement who believes his daughter is attractive enough to have merited my attention. She's a forward little bitch of sixteen, and I wish to reassure her imbecile assumed parent (for the fool has horns a league tall, his fat wife having a lecherous cock-eye for the drunken butler), the girl came to me with as much of a maidenhead as his dishes bear of perfection. True, she brought me a bowl of polenta yesterday morning, for I love the yellow porridge made from the Indian corn which has sucked the sun. I find it excellent when the gums are troublesome, most comforting and warming to the stomach. But yesterday the polenta smelt as if a tom-cat had micturated in the cooking-pot. I was so annoyed I forgot to give her a note I had written to the drunken butler to get me some more of these biscuits I like so much to dip in wine to fortify the stomach. As I sniffed at the piddled polenta, I exclaimed to the girl, 'Maria, what suffering, in the Devil's name, has befallen my polenta?' She stared at me. 'Speak, girl! Speak, speak!'

'I don't know. I expect it is a punishment, my lord,' she replied, sulking with stupid prettiness and oafish cunning.

'That it is,' I agreed, 'but for what?'

'A punishment for what you did to me when you – you know – stole my goodie, and gave me nothing,' she added pointedly.

'Your what?'

'My maidenhead.'

Oh, that it should come to this! 'Now tell the truth, child. Surely I would have had to entertain you a year or two sooner to have been so honoured?'

She is a pretty child though her lovely tight red fat cheeks and round blue eyes suggest more than a touch of stupidity. But at seventy-two one easily forgives the idiocy of pretty girls. Nevertheless I rammed my point home. 'That big ugly footman Hans with the filthy wig has covered you often enough, now has he not?'

The girl stared at me impertinently out of her cool round blue orbs, dropped the dish onto my table with a clatter, and left without a civil word more. Though I am entirely certain that on the occasion she referred to in so unamusing and vulgar a way (her goodie, *goodie* forsooth!), I encountered no virginal resistance in the vicinity of her alleged hymen. Frankly, had I done so in my present reduced circumstance, I would have been forced to retreat. After seventy, one is a coward even if great-spirited still. Of course, this minor question of who did what to which member of the domestic staff would be of little consequence were one certain of the Count's attitude in these matters. But he is entirely directed in such affairs by his major-domo, a curiously untalented old military fool who, after fifty years of service, distinguished himself by retiring from the army as a sub-lieutenant. This cackling and appallingly healthy ass has hated me from the first moment of our meeting, envying my fame and the intimacy it has brought me with the nobility of Europe, among the ranks of whom even our good Count is not especially significant. This Fauchenkircher (repellent and unpronounceable barbarism of a name) has, through these past years, rendered my life unbearable. The Count is away much of the time when I am reduced to eating at the general servants' table to be made the butt of idiotic jokes by the witty major-domo, and, if I wish to escape this privilege, then I must pay for a servant to bring what food this Gadarene permits me, to the library; so I have paid for this benison, encouraging (with infinite subtlety) the service to be executed by young apple-cheeked Maria, from which silly folly this latest question has arisen of whether or not I executed her hymenial goodie. Thus we see that a man is plagued by the results of whatever he does, no matter in which direction he moves, which supports my life-long principle of humble submission to the Divine Will of God; for I am firmly deistic, regardless of what slanderers have said to the contrary, and though I do not always approve of the arrangements of the Almighty, I certainly do not give Him less right to these dispositions than I would give the average stupid absolute monarch. Certainly God rules all, but that is not to say that the task is carried out with much reason or fairness. But as God apparently ignores the depredations of those He has made kings over us here upon earth, so does His Excellency the Count give little attention to his servants'

14

neglect of my most elementary needs. Things were much different when I first accepted his invitation to arrange his unread books. Nothing was too much trouble. Comely girls from the village warmed my sheets. I was a veritable King David; the question now is, does Count Waldstein value me still; or does he not?

I think he does. Only last week he quoted a letter from my dear friend the Prince de Ligne, who confuses me with a peripatetic Jew, but I take no offence. In the same missive, the perceptive princely gentleman had the goodness to observe (clumsily as ever) that 'Casanova is a man without equal, from which each word is a jewel and each thought a book.' Of course, one's wisdom is always inversely proportional to the stupidity of one's audience, and the Prince, being a perfect aristocrat, has considerable gaps in his education. He wrote to me recently (forgetting to enclose the small loan I had requested), 'One is never old with your heart, your genius and your stomach'; but it is precisely the passion of my heart, the depth of my genius and the sensitivity of my stomach which register with astounding accuracy the disgusting certainty of my age. Flattery will no longer stiffen my flaccidity, my lords. The episode with the fat-cheeked minx was, to be honest, an exception, a momentary monument to memory, though in pleasure not to be compared with others too well-remembered. Ah, Memory! Why are you destroying my life?

I have always had a remarkably clear memory; a

capacity to conjure up, quite lucidly, the smallest details of the past. The exact conformation of a hip; the precise creamy consistency of a breast; the particular flavour of a woman; and other affairs less important, such as winning combinations at the table, the arithmetic of chance in a lottery, the odds in favour of my rapier against yours. Throughout my life as a Man (as distinct from a Librarian) I regarded my memory as a talent and a blessing; but lately it returns, great floods of bile drowning my rattish remnants in a book-bound cell, my last imprisonment. I, who have escaped from the prisons of Europe (not to mention the courts which are infinitely more dangerous), I, Giacomo Giralamo Casanova, Chevalier de Seingalt, the only man ever to have escaped from the tightest of them all (I do not mean the Great King's fatal mistress La Pompadour, but the Leads of Venice, the Doge's dread prison), about which adventure you may read in the extremely popular French edition. Well, even then my damned teeth troubled me, and that was years ago. Why should a man of my health and vigour have been so tortured, one of the rare few who has studied the mysteries of diet, frequently curing an attack of the pox in a few weeks by living on salads with my special secret dressing, eschewing both red and white wine, red meat and, of course, women of any colour? But these teeth, damn them, are a joke of the gods; one who has achieved everything by smiling loses his flash, a hero of so much eating, and gnashing, and nibbling, and chewing gently with sensuous mo-

lars, a connoisseur of mouths, finishes his life with his own famous orifice resembling the flabby slit of a gutter-scut. Apparently those who are drawn to sweetness must rot for it; which I regard philosophically as being yet another proof that, if there are any gods, then they can in no way be partisan to our breed; more likely it is that they regard us as silly butterflies whose wings may be collected to embroider kerchiefs for their whores.

It was because of my infernal teeth that I published my famous account of my astonishing escape from the Leads of Venice. There I remarked in the *Avant-Propos* of the French edition, if my memory serves me right, and my memory has ever done so (curse it! For it has become an agony to me; acres of rows of little girls' goodies stretching like lines of split figs to infinity!), I decided then, many years after the events there recorded, to publish what befell me, at the age of thirty, as the divine Dante calls it, *nel mezzo del cammin de nostra vita*. For to tell a story well a man must needs pronounce distinctly; a nimble tongue is not enough, even in love; teeth are indispensable for the utterance of certain consonants which form above a third of the alphabet, and it was, already at thirty, my misfortune to have lost several of mine. However, a man may write well without teeth (or much potency, look at the generality of authors), indispensable as they are to talk. Women detest a toothless man. They know that if the ivory has dropped out of his head, they are most unlikely to find it in his breeches pocket. But as to my incarceration by the Inquisition in the dreaded Leads of Venice: I had been accused of being a notorious magician because of my possession of several works on the subject, forgeries which I hoped to trade sooner or later for a considerable profit to some gullible idiot who believed in such nonsense. I was further accused of disturbing the peace with my sword, though that was certainly not the instrument which had troubled numerous influential husbands of the city. Further accusation: I was heard to call upon, rather than to execrate, the Devil, whenever I lost at gambling. Now I believe that I do call often upon the Devil, but only because I am too polite and considerate to add my small troubles to the conscience of a Divinity who is loaded enough with yours. For ordinary men, confused by the inscrutability of Divine Providence, need must worship it, making their ignorance into a refuge and their helplessness into happiness. For myself, I see

18

God as the Great Gambler who throws us upon the table and, wealthy owner of everything, cares little whether we win or lose. Thus I have observed in my life that good can come out of evil, and evil out of good without any reason at all that one may perceive. All one can do is remain courageous, serving one's own interests as well as one may, for no one and nothing else will do so, and, when good results, thank God (if one is so inclined), bearing in mind that such gratitude is of no consequence to Him whatsover. As I believe I have already said, I am a thorough deist and always have been, as my only theological work, the dialogue between God and myself which I have called *The Dream*, clearly showed to all those many who have read it with fascination. Yet in Venice I was accused of un-Christian behaviour (an irrelevant standard for me), viz. eating meat every day, which I would never do for the sake of my health. It was said, too, that I attended festival Masses in order to spy out lovely women for prey. Well, yes, I preyed upon the praying; does not the Holy Church itself do the same? It was also itemized that I was a Freemason and a spy, and indeed I have been both, as are still so many of our rulers. But to cut a long story short, the Tribunal's police, odious and merciless as their masters, took me about a quarter of an hour before sunrise on a warm July morning as I quitted the Erbaria, the delicious market close to the Rialto where pot-herbs, fruits and flowers disguise the stench of the river, and where men and women who have spent the night in the mad excitement of

19

gaming are in the habit of taking a turn before retiring to bed, often with a newly encountered flower, exotic fruit, or fragrant pot-herb. How well I recall the sweet odour of police entrapment! Shortly I found myself enclosed in a filthy attic lighted only by a small window. That day my jailers brought me, no doubt as an emblem of my punishment, a plate of luke-warm glutinous rice soup and two large, cold religious books.

That night, cramped, I slept upon my left hand on my cot in the Leads. Numbed by the weight of my body, it lost all warmth, movement, sensation, simulating death. The same numbness has often come to me in the cold nights in Dux, reminding me that the first and greatest lesson offered by imprisonment is man's need for philosophy. I had studied deeply, yet had never before had occasion to make use of my learning; but my dead hand recollected me of every motto from every sundial whose shadowy advice of passing time I had ever ignored. And yet, newly escaped from twenty-five thousand companion books, full of excellent mottoes, I still believe that it is better to be ignorant and young, and well-accompanied in a great bed, than old and philosophical in a tomb haunted by crackling parchment voices. Which reminds me, the two great tomes sent by my torturers in the Leads were *The Mystic City* of Sister Maria de Jesus of Agrada, and *The Adoration of the Sacred Heart of Our Lord* by a canting wretch of a Jesuit named Caravida. Odd how one remembers such details, but there it is. Oh, I can tell you, one needed all

20

one's philosophy to survive such stuff! At least in Duchkov I have made certain that we are free of the maniac follies of mad nuns and creeping priests, restoring reason to His Lordship's library by casting out all such insane melancholy life-detesting devils masquerading as the voices of God. There is now hardly a holy book to be found there, and it has become a good library full of those excellent bad books which free the mind and soul of man. But who can read even the best of books with dogs barking through the night?

All night, every night, these filthy eternally mat-ing canines (for I swear that unlike dogs in the rest of the world, the hounds of Duchkov like Man are not restricted in their season) yodel at me. I com-plained to that stinking groom with the filthy wig, Hans, the grasper of goodies. But to what purpose? Count Waldstein, like all true aristocrats, loves dogs better than people. No doubt the rascally groom reported my disaffection for His Grace's

21

shuddering flea-bitten creatures. That might have been even more damaging than an intrusion on his seigneurial rights over the grubby girls of Duchkov. For did I not say in front of that treacherous fellow that I would not have His Lordship's favourite bitch Venus for a collar to my old coat? Yes, the Devil take them all, that could explain why, when there were more guests than usual last Thursday at dinner, His Excellency's librarian, Jacques Casanova, Chevalier de Seingalt, a Kabbalist who will never grow old and suchlike cat's flux, was placed at a small side-table. It raises a troublesome question for which I would rather not find an answer, for whose dog, I wonder, am I become? Devil help me, if my breast were hairless, I would have packed my petticoats long ago. The noble idiot has tired of my slack old wisdom. I certainly have, so why not he? I must go (I decided), before I am cast out. And yet where to go? I have come to detest travel, once my second greatest pleasure. The parsimonious Fauchenkircher keeps Count Waldstein's castle cold as the anus of my life; must I disappear down it?

Of course, it might have been the matter of the girl and her goodie, though what is another hymen to the grand Waldstein with his great annual gathering of such by seigneurial right? The Count teases me often on this matter, maintaining that he has, by tradition and legal right, more girls in his harem than ever I could have acquired in mine. Then he laughs a great deal however I may answer, for I dare not say I would never in my time have given a bent florin for all his dubious virgins, for this would be too insulting; on the other hand, if I express admiration of this hymenial benefit of his great position, would it not imply a degree of envy? Then Fauchenkircher's cunning would transform into Casanovan plots to steal these desirable fruits from the Waldstein orchard. The Count would laugh a little less often if he know that I knew that his prowess with the fair sex is not very impressive for a descendant of the great General Wallenstein. I heard this of a lady to whom he had paid assiduous court, but I will not write down the shameful details. In any case, failure in these matters does not prevent a man from being eager to fail yet again. As to the kitchen-girl in question, was her flavour one he looked forward to, I wonder? Supposing I have sampled a seigneurial delicacy and marked a Waldstein goodie with the Casanovan seal of approval, and he knows and hates me for it? By Satan's horns – I am finished! I must pull my old bones and infernal false teeth together, pack up my trinkets and memories and leave. And so I have, damn you all to Hell! I have vacated the pigsty. I shall now drink another bottle of this appalling plum-brandy and fly off unaided by any mechanical means whatsoever.

'Another bottle of your disgusting brandy, Ssstichka!' I called, my teeth leaping out as they will occasionally, though I have never in all my travels seen a better set than that tooth-doctor in Strasburg made me for forty ducats, a great deal of money, but worth it, for apart from an occasional hiss and the odd jump, it is scarcely noticeable that they are false. This brandy is, without doubt, the water of life of this derelict country. It puts blood in the heart, and the heart leaps again. Perhaps I should renegotiate my contract with the Count, make my conditions very clear indeed, as my old friend the penniless Baron Tiretta, whose only asset was the largest penis in Paris, did with that wealthy old Duchess. He lived well for several years, and inherited a comfortable competence upon the good lady's death, which was occasioned by a surfeit of amusement following upon oysters cooked in Marsala with a rich dressing of shrimps to which she was most partial. But my whoredom to the Count Waldstein has brought me no excess of oysters or amusement, only purulent polenta, micturated macaroni and the shrimps of a little trollop who, whether or not she had a virginity, certainly had crabs. But I assure you, my lord, the girl was not *intacta* at the time. I have saved your lordship considerable embarrassment. Your groom with the filthy wig had evacuated into your little *olla-podrida* of a scullery maid, rendering her quite unsuitable for seigneurial honours. Trust my expertise in such matters, sir. The whole world knows that in affairs concerning goodies and their disposal the word of Casanova is paramount. Why should I not simply insist upon my status in such matters – as when I persuaded him that the disposal of that great tonnage of religious mediocrity in his library was an essential first step towards the creation of a monument to Reason and Intellect? I came at him with such rapier-pointed arguments that his brain, which, in its pure aristocracy can hardly be equalled, grew fuddled. 'Well, well, Casanova,' he chuckled, laughing as he always does when unable to cope with intellectual activities more demanding than shooting off the goodies of innumerable inedible and harmless small birds, 'well, well, Casanova, you had better do as you think best. But I shall miss the presence of some of these old friends.'

He will miss them! As if he ever had read anything more elevating than a court journal or a dirty story! But His Excellency can always be persuaded by an opposing will that is determined upon its course; except in the matter of money. This, indeed, is why his wretched servants have such an absurd degree of influence over him, for he pays them nothing, and therefore must regard them, winking at their vices. Thus his execrable cooks steals unrestrictedly from the kitchen purse, his loathsome groom has his will of the entire establishment while stealing oats, and Fauchenkircher drinks the best wine with his sotted friends. Meanwhile the Chevalier de Seingalt is fed pestilential polentas daily and is ignored at a side-table. Casanova at a side-table! How to bear such ignominy? I who escaped from the dreaded Leads of Venice, the only human being in history ever to have done so, as all may read in the many editions of my account which have appeared, most of them pirated, paying me not a penny. I presented a French copy to the library of Dux. His Excellency is always boasting of having read it, though I do not believe him; even the study of the genealogy of a prize bitch exhausts him after the first three sirings. The poor nobleman's memory is not good, for His Excellency of Waldstein is committed by his own unbreachable word to pay me an insignificant salary regularly, and I have not been in receipt of it for several years, though I am presented constantly with filthy bits of paper with appallingly written accounts of my expenses. No doubt I am expected to finance the feeding of the dogs that their barking may not decrease, and the health of the cats who supervise the preparation of my polenta. Formerly, of course, I cared nothing even for considerable expenses such as forty ducats for my teeth which occasionally hiss like the mice whispering to each other in the wainscot when disturbed by the nocturnal scratching of my quill. I trained a mouse a year or so ago to take crumbs from a corner of my desk. But I inadvertently fed it a little weevily macaroni one night, and the creature left me in disgust. Possibly he died beneath the collected works of Ariosto, for I noticed subsequently an unpleasant smell emanating from those volumes which would have been more appropriate to a theological work by a deranged nun; but there are no such atrocities remaining in my library.

I should like so much from time to time to send a little money to one or two poor creatures now, lovely children once, who still write to me of their unforgettable love and their need for immediate assistance. But my means are so restricted. The Count is my debtor, and his servants continue their uncontrolled stealing from the household purse. I only wish I could lay my hands on it. I have tried to persuade His Honour into a magical enterprise, a sure means of profit. I mentioned recently that the vibrations of the Elixir of Life were, I felt by my astrological calculations, especially amenable to the latitude of his castle at Duchkov, and that it would at least invigorate his potency, if not, assuredly, extend his life. But no, His Excellency, who formerly protested when we first met in Teplitz, his great interest in Alchemy and the Stone and my skill in such secrets, is grown wary of me. Rich and wary is a most vulgar combination and isolates me in this savage guttural country where every word sounds like the bubbling cough of one dying from the plethora which, amazingly, I did not contract in the dreaded Leads of Venice. Even here in dreadful Duchkov my chest has remained quite clear of pleurisy, and I sleep well, only not at night, though the brandy (local infusion of the piss of stallions) has made me feel warm and drowsy. Watching the fire as it burns low, painting faces and the haunches of women and horses in the glowing embers, I half-dream of a day I described in some detail in my Memoirs, for it was the day when my true life began.

I was eight. I stood in the corner of a room supporting my head, my eyes fixed upon a stream of blood flowing from my nose to the floor; for I often had nosebleeds and was considered a child of thick and stupid disposition. So my grandmother Marzia took me by gondola to Muran, to the wretched hovel of an old woman who sat on a rickety bed, a black cat in her arms and half-a-dozen more purring around her while my grandmother talked to her in the patois of Forli about me. The witch nodded and grandmother Marzia gave her a silver coin, whereupon she opened a large box, lifted me, and dropped me in it, (was I destined to always find myself in prisons?). She locked it, calling to me not to be frightened. I was stupefied, but I kept quiet, holding a handkerchief to my nose because it was still bleeding; otherwise I was very indifferent to the uproar going on outside – for I could hear laughter, weeping, singing, screams, shrieks, and knocking which shook the box. At last the blood stopped flowing and I was taken out. The wonderful old witch lavished caresses upon me, took off my clothes, lay me on the bed, and burnt some drugs, gathering the smoke in a sheet which she wrapped around me. She pronounced many strange incantations, then took off the sheet, and gave me five delicious sugar-plums. She rubbed my temples and the nape of my neck with an ointment which exhaled a delightful perfume; I was sad when she finally clothed me again. She told me that my haemorrhages would soon leave me for ever, and swore me for my own safety to secrecy for, as I came later to know only too well, the great State of Venice had a way with witches. After having sworn me, she told me a beautiful lady would pay me a visit the following night; she would make me wonderfully happy, and for all my life watch over me; I would be her best-beloved. Then, my grandmother fussing over me, we returned home.

That night I fell asleep almost as soon as I was in bed, without giving a thought to the beautiful visitor I was to receive; but, waking up a few hours later, I saw, coming down the chimney, a dazzling woman, wearing a splendid dress with immense hoops, on her head a crown set with precious stones, which sparkled with brilliant fire. Slowly she approached, her majestic but kind countenance smiling gently. She bent over me, and her breath was sweet, and then, like a cloud of perfume, she sank down upon me. She brought several small beautiful boxes out of her pocket, and slowly emptied their contents like shining stars over my head, softly whispering blessings. Then after uttering a long speech, not a single word of which I understood, she kissed me with passionate tenderness and disappeared the same way she had come. Sublimely happy, I soon sank into a perfect profound sleep, the deepest of my life.

The next morning, my grandmother came to dress me. She, too, cautioned me to be silent, threatening me with death if I dared speak of my night's adventures. This command, laid upon me by the first woman ever to have complete authority over me, caused me to store my vision under a seal of secrecy, in the most inmost depths of my dawning memory. In any case, I had no one to talk to of it for my disease had rendered me dull and retired;

29

my life was considered likely to be but a short one. As to my parents, they were handsome theatricals who could not bring themselves to speak to me.

After the journey to Muran, and the nocturnal visit of the fairy, I continued to bleed from the nose, but less every day. My memory quickly developed, and I learned to read in less than a month. It would be ridiculous, of course, to attribute this extraordinary cure to magic, but strange elements were undeniably present at Muran. As for my beautiful queen, I have always considered her to be a dream of perfect womanhood with her mysterious powers of love and death. Oh, come to me again, great Goddess, come to me now, vision of all women, Dream of Destiny, dazzling apparition; blind me again with the brilliance of the reflected suns of an endless future! Come to me, sweet Queen, or, considering my present inelegant condition and unpleasing circumstances, at least send some magical messenger bearing good news about any damn thing at all in this cold, foetid, miserable, ageing world!

(II)

*I observed a tall ancient man,
his strangely noble head
bent in thought*

'YOUR HONOUR'S boots are ready.' Stichka's rasping voice awoke me. He held the boots forward so that I could see readily that the soles and heels were perfectly repaired, shaped and stitched most carefully, not at all the crude work of the local bumpkins. Stichka, too, was impressed. 'This Jew-fellow does a fine job. Will your excellency try them on?'

I leaned forward, feeling my wig awry. I straightened it and held my feet, gnarled bundles of veins, forward. The boots slipped on easily, bringing manly support to my scrawny limbs. I stood up (with Stichka's help). I shook off the brandy and the sleep and felt a fine power spreading up my legs. It briefly occurred to me that should it ascend above the knees, I might find myself well and truly back in the saddle again. Indeed, I seemed to feel a powerful irradiation ascending my body and percolating through the thickened passages into my vitals.

'By the saints and Holy Virgin, you look truly fine, Signor Casanova!' Stichka said with surprise but genuine admiration.

The brandy and the little rest had revived me. I felt in my pocket for a coin or two. 'Pay the cobbler.' I held forward the money, a generous fee, but well-deserved.

Stichka shook his head. 'I have already offered him money, but he will take nothing for the work.'

I frowned. My own resources were thin enough in truth, but could I as a gentleman accept a gift from an itinerant artisan? Clearly I could not. 'Where is this proud cobbler?' I asked.

'In the kitchen, sir. He walks around the table a good deal, sleeps not at all, takes no refreshment and will not be paid.'

'We shall soon remedy the last of his disorders,' I muttered and made my way most comfortably, my feet warm and nurtured as two beloved babes in their swaddling clothes.

In the kitchen by the light of the guttering fire I observed a tall, ancient man, bearded, wearing a reddish caftan and a short woollen cloak, pacing, his strangely noble head bent in thought, about a large heavy table on which was mounted, cold and congealed, the hindquarters of a roasted pig. He wore sandals upon his bare feet and occasionally muttered some query to himself.

'Well, sir shoe-maker,' I said after a few moments in which he seemed quite unaware of my presence, 'you have done my feet a favour and I would reward you for it.'

He started and looked towards me blankly as if unable to understand my German. Then he replied in perfect Italian with the barest trace of an indistinguishable accent. 'You owe me nothing, Signor Casanova.' His voice was deep, his delivery slow,

34

his expression still and serious. 'But you may, if you will, give three small coins to the poor.'

'That I will do gladly,' I said, puzzled by both his request and his demeanour, for he had about him a quality of grandeur which one hardly expects to find among leather-workers. 'But surely the labourer is worthy of his hire, and I would feel at a loss paying you nothing for yours. Will you at least drink with me?'

'Thank you, but I will neither eat nor drink.' The strange fellow continued his peregrination of the table as if the unfortunate subject of a compelling tic.

'You await the post-chaise?' I asked. 'Do you travel far?'

'Very far,' he replied, looking at me sharply.

'I, too, wish to leave this totally dispensable township well behind me. So you know me, sir?'

'The innkeeper spoke your name, and who is there who does not know of your extraordinary escape from the Leads of Venice?'

'Ah, yes,' I replied, 'that impossible escape embellishes me, a unique award by Our Lady of Destiny.'

Stichka was standing by, listening carefully and snatching up the occasional word. 'Ah, yes,' he coughed in German, 'the Leads! Mention Casanova anywhere and the greatest fools know how he escaped from the Doge's prison and screwed the world's wives.' He wheezed out a bellyful of beer breath.

'Even here, you observe, in bastard Bohemia, in

dirty Dux, I am famous,' I said. 'Breathe in the opposite direction, Stichka, if you please. Do you speak French, sir?'

'I do.' The old man (for he was older than I) replied in that language.

'Well, Stichka doesn't,' I continued. 'Do you know, sir,' I sat down upon a bench against the wall, 'when first I came to this Duchkov,' (Stichka blew in disgust and left us) 'I was accorded by the noble Count and his grubby dependants and lousy powdered friends the greatest respect. They anticipated that I would reveal to them the secret of the Philosopher's Stone. I would demonstrate methods whereby their crumbling *schlosses* would be rebuilt with gold. I would devise and establish for the benefit of their greed a Bohemian lottery in which they would all take shares and be feloniously issued with winning tickets, for they were eager for entirely new methods of stealing from the oafish peasants and turgid citizenry of their provinces. I would regale them with endless spicy stories from my Memoirs, reform their debased and unspeakable cuisine, and teach them manners. In which regard my solitary suggestion to His Excellency was rejected, for I opined that one does not sneeze snuff into the silver bowl from which one's guest is served with mouldy punch; but he continued to sneeze all over me. The wine here, you know, is indistinguishable from vinegar. But their plumbrandy, though violent and noxious, keeps out the cold. Well, sir, where was I? Yes – the academicians of the province prevailed upon me to make a scientific examination of the reform of the calendar. So I began my work of civilizing boring Bohemia, and soon every peasant in the country trembled knowing that a great magician resided at Duchkov. But I would sooner have them fear me than love me, for a little affection here costs endless bribes which I simply do not have available at the present time.

'Does His Excellency realize that if I had had available to me reasonable funds, I would have long ago been away, high over the turrets of Duchkov like a tattered carrion crow searching the green patchwork of the world for some comforting cadaver of the past on which to feed my declining years? Of course, he knows that had I the funds I would have left his library to the worms. That is why, of course, he has not paid me my pitiful stipend. As for my attempts to gain a little help from wealthy friends of the past, they have been contemptibly received. Take the Princess Lobkowitz, who once would have torn the gems from her throat to satisfy my least desire; I wrote to her some touching nonsense about my dog having died and the ensuing loneliness of Duchkov growing unbearable to me. How I longed for adequate arrangements to be made for me to be received in some warm and stimulating court! The lady wrote back: "Monsieur, having learnt of the death of your well-loved greyhound, I send you the gift of a little dog, knowing that she will nowhere be better cared for than with you, Monsieur. I hope with all my heart that she has all the qualities which may, in

37

some fashion, help you forget the deceased." The little bitch now whores nightly with His Excellency's hounds and the ensuing baying would keep me awake were I able to sleep. The Princess Lobkowitz, incidentally, throws away more at the gaming tables in one month than it would take to keep me in luxury, with several little dogs, for the rest of my life. I ignored her letter and her snuffling gift, but perhaps I should write to her again. "Madame, I sit here alone in the night except for the company of your well-loved little dog who licks my hand as I write to you, an ageing deserted gentleman who longs for a warmer climate and the comforts of a simple elegant life anywhere other than in Duchkov." No doubt she would send me a cat.'

Throughout my endless diatribe the strange fellow had peregrinated the kitchen table with its

obscene decoration of cold larded pork, occasionally glancing towards me with large, dark sympathetic eyes. Nevertheless I felt a certain embarrassment. 'Forgive me, sir,' I said, wiping my nose which, with the sadness of my soliloquy, had run somewhat freely. 'The pleasure of hearing good French spoken after so long has made me run on thoughtlessly. But sir, do not joke with me further. You are surely no Jew, but some travelling gentleman with a fine knowledge of languages, I perceive, and an eccentric hobby. My good friend the Prince de Ligne insists upon winding the many clocks in his palace himself. I knew once a noble gentleman in Venice who baked his own bread. So you, sir, making the grand tour, amuse yourself by simulating a shoe-maker, though one may tell at once from the fineness of your work that you are no mere artisan. Tell me, sir, do I have you right?'

'Yes and no,' the fellow replied with that parsimony of explanation which makes so many unusual people disappointing conversationalists.

'*Yes*, I would hazard,' I continued, 'in so far as I am speaking to a gentleman, for I have that nobility inherent in me which makes me sensible of breeding in another. And *no*, I would guess, in so far as you practise this small but skilful trade as a means of sustenance, but wish to compliment me with the gift of your skill.'

I laughed nervously, for my companion was staring at me with a fixed expression of indescribable regret. 'I remember once,' I continued hurriedly, hoping to relieve the strange sense I had of

39

some ancient mute appeal never answered, 'when I was regarded as a great magician who had escaped from the most inescapable jails, the most importunate ladies and the most infuriate husbands, with the aid of Satan rather than by the exercise of simple intelligence, I once financed a rapid exit from Madrid by selling a charming little chamois purse made by the same gypsy who factored these very boots I wear, now perfected again by your skill. A pretty little purse it was, embellished with a large "F" in gold thread and complete with five small silver coins of Moorish origin, obviously the veritable lucky purse of Fortunatus which is never empty. Your carelessness for money would suggest that your own purse on your belt there, with no distinguishing sign upon it, is the very original, mocking my pretty forgery.'

'I am indeed sufficiently provided for,' the stranger replied.

I laughed a little shrilly and quaffed a glass of brandy in one. 'Ah! Would I could say the same! But I must admit, my magic has grown a little impotent with the years. I confess my present inability to conjure up even a small cacodemon capable of advancing me to a warmer clime. Yet the servants here are still quite convinced that I am a warlock. That dirty groom accused me yesterday of magicking his horses so that they became fretful. Yet it is obvious that he has been feeding them mouldy oats and selling the better part of their feed. But supposing he tells his absurd story to the Count? You expect His Lordship to reject such an absurd suggestion. And yet the thought planted in his poor thick Germanic head will be watered by tales of my prodigious deeds in the past; and people have always attributed my fortune to the Devil rather than to my own abilities and talents. That way they are able to feel less inferior to one who, defeated only by age, is reduced to complaining about the scandalous behaviour of servants and the dubious favour of a grubby, tale-bearing, false virgin. Her alleged father, a distinguished chef, you understand, annoys our master's major-domo, the aged drunken sub-lieutenant Fauchenkircher, by retailing my complaints concerning the polenta and the macaroni, not to mention the invariably sour milk, and coffee like the granulated contents of an ancient jakes.

'That foul groom, Hans, who I believe has the kitchen girl nightly, always gives me a bad horse if I wish to ride a little. Not that I do very often, but occasionally, for the illusion of freedom from the leaking walls of Duchkov, I take a little ride, at considerable cost to my piles, not to mention the torment to my ears of the endless blasting of His Excellency's perpetual hunting horns. And what of this (listen to this unbearable insult, I have not yet mentioned it to His Excellency), his own ignorant priest, a confessor with a great deal to confess, let me tell you, has had the audacity to try and convert me! Convert *me* who had my theological training at the knees of cardinals and the feet of the Pope in Rome, this ignorant German country priest tries to convert the author of the deistic classic *The Dream*!

41

But now, without further ado, let me come to the worst of it, for this, sir, is definitive. The Count did not anticipate my morning greeting yesterday. I said to him, "Good morning, Count, I trust you have slept well?" Normally he laughs and replies, "Good morning, Casanova. I trust you have not slept alone?" and he says it *before* I have spoken. Yesterday he merely grunted and hurried on, no jokes, no laughter! Well, it is clear. Fauchenkircher has been lying again. Why, otherwise, was there a delay over serving me wine last night? I was served wine last but one of all at the table, and I was *not* introduced to that so-called distinguished personage, a little German princeling with an enormously long moustache, who has come to see a lance alleged to have pierced the side of Jesus. Everyone else, heavy stupid neighbours, von this and von that, was introduced to this noble little Teutonic excrescence, but not I. Why? Why? Oh, God, yes – it must be true! The Count is sickened by my age and the mumbling of my wretched new teeth which cost forty ducats and were specially tailored, a pox on all dental carpenters, thieves and tricksters grown rich by the pains in the world's mouth! I would I could draw out, one by one, with broken pincers, the fangs of the incompetent wolf who planted these insane champers within my head! Satan damn them! They are flying loose again!'

My teeth at this point sprang out and fell upon the table, fastening themselves ravenously in the cold backside of the roast pig. As I retrieved and delarded them, the stranger quietly observed in Latin, 'I have never found a shortage of thieves and tricksters anywhere in the world.'

I replaced my teeth. They tasted of roast pork. Perhaps I would take a slice or two later. 'These Princes, sir,' I assured my companion, 'these German Princes are the greatest thieves, the ignorant little farts. Take this distinguished Teutonic anus recently honouring us with his presence. The Count lent him books without informing me. There are twenty-five thousand volumes in my library; I have spent some thirteen years cataloguing them, and the good, the *puissant*, the generous and intelligent Count Waldstein takes volumes out of their correct positions and lends them to German princelings whose ability to read is unlikely to equal their talent for growing hair on their slobbering upper lips. As for this present lordling, he looks like a naked ageing whore standing on her head, the ludicrous midget. But, item one, the Count lends books without reference to his distinguished librarian without whose work his only monument would be the enormous number of idiot children in Duchkov.'

My companion interjected. 'I have never found a shortage of idiots anywhere in the world. They balance the tricksters and thieves, which is said to exemplify God's harmony in all things.'

'And no doubt,' I exclaimed, 'they everywhere blame Casanova for the surplus of the one and the rogueries of the other! Do you know, sir, that even here where the only seigneurial obligation conscientiously fulfilled by my lord of Waldstein is the impregnation of his pretty little virgin *(soi-disant)* sows, that whenever a girl becomes pregnant, the first speculation is whether or not it is the work of Casanova? I ask you, sir, to witness. I am seventy-two and have a troublesome bladder disorder. If I could rely upon my withered instrument merely to piss regularly, I would be deeply grateful. And still they will have me the king of cuckold-makers. And now this comic little Waldstein believes it, too. I must convince him it was the groom that first docked his kitchen maid, this same groom who did not touch his hat to me yesterday. And there you have it. That's what Casanova has come to. And that smelly-bearded little aristocrat turdling had the audacity to laugh at my German speech! (Filthy language for a filthy people!) And the Count laughed with him! Devil take me for an old ordure! Damn and double damn me! Fools laugh at my German! Cats piss in my polenta! It is too much to bear! I am old, old, old!'

I attribute the passion into which I now delivered myself to the anxieties and miseries of my situation, the lateness of the hour, deprivation of sleep, imbibing of strong drink upon an empty stomach, and that bitter bile which arises from an ancient and unhappy soul when its owner considers the short, black, lonely journey before him. So this mother rose in me as I considered, with mounting excitement, the injustices and loathsome realities of my situation, deprived of respect, the least comfort resented, the smallest pleasure withheld. I rose to my feet and shook my gouty fists at Fate. Hot tears gushed from my bloodshot eyes. Anger at the world, pity for myself, and hatred of old age, pursued one another. In my mind a black dog chased a black cat which stalked a black rat, but none of them pounced upon anything but emptiness. And so I fell to the filthy floor and the darkness fell upon me.

How long I lay there I cannot say for it seemed like the eternity of death, but I believe it was, in fact, not long before my eyes opened. Descending through the mist above me I distinguished the old Jew, his hands spread before him as he recited strange words. My head rapidly clearing, I quickly recognized the posture of his hands to be that of the Kabbalistic blessing, and, while not comprehending his words, recognized them well enough to be some style of Hebrew. I sat up as quickly as I could, alarmed that some magic was being worked upon me. 'Permit me,' the stranger said as he observed my movement with a compassion I found unnecessarily patronizing, 'allow me, sir, to offer a protective blessing. You were for some moments possessed of the demon of misery. I am hopeful that my poor skill has helped to exorcize the spirit.' He helped me to my feet.

'Pass me that filthy brandy, if you will be so good,' I requested him, and as I drank from the bottle found myself already returning to my normal frame of mind wherein I wondered what esoteric or arcane knowledge might be gleaned from this fellow. For I have always been opportunistic in all such situations, often profiting from the most adverse of circumstances and so extending my understanding of the mysterious forces to which man's life is as helplessly subject as dice are to Destiny. I handed the bottle to the stranger. 'I note that you are some kind of master,' I said. 'I have always accounted myself a student of such matters, so tell me, who are your masters, oh master? I myself am familiar with the *Key of Solomon* and have read in German the *Book of the Sacred Magic of Abra-Melin*.'

The stranger sniffed scornfully. 'The so-called *Clavicula Salomonis* is not of true Kabbalistic origin and is, in my opinion, a merely popular and unconsiderable mess of rubbish. As to *Abra-Melin*, I can personally assure you that its alleged author, the so-called Abraham the Jew of Worms, did not exist, although I will agree that its perpetrator knew Hebrew unusally well for a German.'

Perceiving that I was, indeed, in the presence of a serious exponent of the subject, I decided that a modest approach would befit me best. 'I have only

encountered the great *Book of Splendour* incidentally in the course of my alchemical researches,' I
confessed with disarming honesty. 'You are no
doubt familiar with the work of the unparalleled
Joseph Taitazah, who identified alchemy with the
Divine wisdom of the Kabbalah. Furthermore, I
expect you have considered the writing of Hayyim
Vital, who spent two years of his youth studying
alchemy and composed a most revealing book upon
its practices.'

'Vital publicly repented of this indiscretion in his
old age,' responded the stranger, wiping his nose
upon the sleeve of his caftan. 'One must remember
always in this discussion the basic symbolical difference between the two sciences; for while the
alchemist considers gold to be perfection, the
Kabbalist regards it as *Din*, with a lower rank than
silver, which is *Hesed*.' He glared at me with
triumphant challenge as if demanding that I deny
his knowledge.

'Well, of course,' I responded, 'that is so, and
understandably, for according to *Portae Lucis*,
Kabbalah is *luna*, whereas alchemy favours *sol*.'

'In the Latin translation to which you refer,
Paulus Ricius frequently mis-translates the original
author J. Gikatilla, whose *Sha'arei Orah* makes it
clear that Kabbalah is concerned with the marriage
of sun and moon symbolizing the union of Torah
and Shekinah, rather than their opposition.'

I could tell by now that I was in the presence of
one whose mastery of the sacred art was truly
considerably more advanced than my own, and so,

47

having put my man to the test and found him promising, I now decided to pursue my own interest in such matters. 'May I conclude, sir,' I asked him casually, 'that your studies have been in the realm of what the great Maimonides describes as "practical Kabbalah", the same being theurgical, the adept pursuing the magical use of the Sacred Names rather than passive meditation upon them?'

'You speak, I take it, of what the Abulafian school calls *hokhma ha-shimmush*,' the Jew snapped back at me, 'which, as you perhaps know, is the Hebrew expression for the technical Greek term "praxis", denoting magical activity.'

Hoping that I was not to be encumbered here by mere pedantry, I hastened to assure the stranger that yes, indeed, it was practical magical activity with which I had always been concerned.

'There is, of course, a great difference between the *shimmusha rabba*, "the great theurgy", and the "little theurgy", the *shimmusha zutta*,' he opined.

'Indeed there is,' I agreed, 'for the great theurgy offers (I read in Moses de Leon) mastership over the names and the ability to thread them into formulae which may alter the state of a man. Is that not so, master?' My heart trembled with excitement as I asked this not entirely theoretical question.

The Jew glowered at me, a concentrated stare in the theatrical style adopted by many tricksters I have known, whose methods I have, from time to time, myself utilized. Yet I did not wish to call the bluff upon the stranger. Magic of the Kabbalah has

48

been practised for some five hundred years, perhaps longer, and there cannot be such an amount of confusing smoke without some small fire of veracity burning somewhere. Who could say that this fellow had not been sent to me in my time of crisis with some power to improve my future? 'Master,' I said with grovelling respect, the posture required by all magi, 'will you not speak?'

A deep sigh issued from his throat, and raising his right hand, he traced about my figure a protective line in the air. 'I see about you,' he orated in *basso profundo*, 'the ether of the *zelen* by which a man is surrounded. By its blue light I am able to read your soul. It is seriously shrunken to the size of a dried black pea. I must warn you that it may soon decompose into a little dust to be blown away by the winds of your own anger.'

'Your vision does not surprise me, master,' I replied, showing no contempt for the idiocy of his aura-perception. I am familiar with those tricks of fortune-telling in which a man is convinced that he may see (with the aid of mirrors) his own form standing before him and relating his future. I consider all such games to be arrant chicanery, yet I remained hopeful that the mysterious stranger would prove himself to be of serious substance. 'I have suffered greatly in recent years,' I encouraged him. 'Such experiences shrink the soul. Are there not words, keys to the doors of past and future which may readmit one into better times?'

'Many of the masters travelled in time,' the

stranger replied. 'Some of them voyaged even to the abode of the rebel angels Aza and Azael in the mountains of darkness to study under their black auspices. There they ate of the leaves of the Tree of Knowledge and thus journeyed into the past and future.'

'Can you assist an eager scholar to pursue such journeys?' I insisted hopefully.

'I can,' he replied, 'but I will not. For it is the praxis of the false science of the Orientals which mixeth the clean with the unclean together. Such mixtures are unstable and may cause harmful explosions.'

This kind of mystical talk always irritates me, but still I possessed myself in patience. 'Will you then practise the mystic secret of writing the future with no hand or pen?' I implored him, 'or, at least, levitate for good faith the table over there? I have often read in the ducal library specific instructions for such demonstrations of power. Or perhaps you have a divining rod in your bag. Or possibly you are familiar with invocations which may cure unpleasant conditions. I have several, and any small relief to my situation would be most gratefully received.'

'In the sapphiric ether that surrounds you, all that has happened is simultaneously present,' he informed me; which information was not exactly of earth-shattering novelty to me, for after twelve years of writing one's Memoirs, one knows that the past hangs around whether or not its ether is sapphiric.

'I understand very well what you say, master,' I replied, swallowing my impatience. 'Continue if you will.'

'The book in which all your deeds now and to come are expressly written down and all your movements recorded is with you, open to be read.' The stranger pursued his point.

'But I am asking, sir, if one may return in substance to what one remembers,' I insisted edgily.

'By all means,' he replied calmly. 'You have only to read from the book the words appropriate to the required time of your life.'

'Well then, sir, let us cease this fascinating but endless discussion,' I exclaimed, 'and for God's sake, or the Devil's, read it!'

The stranger shook his head, deprecating my passion. 'You must read it yourself,' he said sadly, infuriating me.

'Then tell me in the name of Hell,' I howled, 'how, how?'

The old man proceeded, ignoring my outburst. 'Abulafia offers instructions to those who wish to return to their youth as dogs to their vomit. I perceive your haste and lust to do so and ask you, sir, to reconsider.'

'Please,' I begged him with true sincerity, 'please, if you can assist me out of this foul jakes of age, do so, I implore you, do it now!' Tears sped from my eyes again, and I felt as weak as a discarded woman.

'You wish to return, I take it,' he said, unmoved

by my suffering, 'to former moments of pleasure and victory. Of course you do. It is the torture of old age to dwell upon such memories. Well, sir, you may do so, but I must warn you that wherever you travel in the past, your mind and spirit will remain of the present.'

'But what could be better?' I exclaimed delightedly. 'My mature experience, my wisdom, my understanding of the world, my polished intelligence, my highly educated spirit, all contained in a better-fitted lodging. In the names of all the demons and the angels, I take it on without complaint. Old Casanova's mind and spirit in young Casanova's body! It is the dream of every man! Do it, sir, do it, recite your names, intone your incantations, instruct me the way out of this cloaca of life, and take as reward whatever I have, even to that dilapidated piece of merchandise I call my soul!' I grabbed his arm in my excitement.

'I ask no reward,' the old man replied firmly withdrawing my hand. 'This collecting of souls is a Christian business, a matter in which my own tendency is sceptic for I myself believe this notion of the soul to be a compensation Man offers himself for the inevitability of death. He longs to be convinced that, after his final breath, there is still an existence for him. No, sir, I believe firmly that there is no life after death, although I can witness (as you can yourself) that life may be over-extended most tediously. Ah, if you were interested, sir, I could tell you a story that would shrivel your heart.'

But I, caring nothing for the old fool's reminiscences, interrupted him rudely, begging him to get to the point. 'To the point, sir!' I cried. 'Let us hear your interesting memoirs on some other occasion. For the present, I am the subject in hand. In the name of the Tetragrammaton, tell me how am I to proceed? What are the instructions of the divine Abulafia? There is a volume or two of his in the library. I would I had studied them seriously.'

'As you wish, sir,' the stranger replied mildly. 'But bear my advice in mind and remember that you may at any time open the door to your return should you so desire it –'

'Are you mad?' I cried. 'Tell me what to do, I conjure you, for I have no fears. Lay on!'

The old man looked about the foul kitchen with acute distaste. 'For the Abulafian formula to work well, we should be in a better place, clean, well-lit with many candles. Thou shouldst cleanse thy body and thy clothes, thy garments should be white, for brightness is helpful in leading the heart towards the fear and love of God's power.'

'And then? And then?'

'Then on clean paper combine a few or many letters, permuting them until thy heart be warm. Then be mindful of their movements and of what thou canst bring forth from them.'

'What then?'

'When thou feelest that thy heart is truly warm, thou shalt see that by combination of the letters thou canst travel wheresoever thou wilt. Turn then thy whole mind upon thy purpose. Meditate

53

deeply as thy tablet and quill drop from thy hand, and thy soul beginneth its travels. And now, from the strong intellectual influx within thee, thy whole body will be seized by an extremely strong trembling, so that thou wilt think that surely thou art about to die, because it is then that thy soul, overjoyed with its knowledge, will leave thy body to go whither it will. What ails you, Signor Casanova?'

Well may he ask, for I was already following his instructions in my mind with the greatest intensity. So determined was I for any form of escape, that numbers danced before me and led me rapidly past the years to an evening in Venice before the dreaded Doge's revenge fell upon me, a time of such sweetness that I must hurry there. And so hurry I did. My entire body shook as if seized by an ague. My false denture chattered to my true teeth. The hair upon my neck stood on end. My hands shook as my body rattled like an old carriage being pulled by a team of mighty horses.

'I see the power is upon you,' the stranger observed after watching me silently for a few moments. 'Abulafia notes such effects and recommends that you place your hands upon your knees and your head between them.'

With his help, I did so, and my transportation proceeded more comfortably.

I found myself in Venice in church upon a holy day. My dress was exceptionally fine, and I had that sense of well-being that comes from excellent

health together with the confidence which proceeds from one's youth having been well-spent in
learning highly educational vices. The service was
proceeding with a plethora of angelic choiring,
mounting to some high point in the theatrical
entertainment, but I was aware of nothing and no
one other than a certain ardent little nun. Several
elegant ladies, dressed to bemuse, had flung most
speaking *oeillades* in my direction, but I had al-
lowed them to fall harmlessly at my feet (shod most
beautifully), and there they lay ignored; for my
whole attention was upon this slim figure in black
who followed the service with such utter devotion;
or did her eyes stray from time to time in my
direction? I had observed the young nun upon
entering the cathedral where my intention had
been to seek out possible new conquests among

the fashionable ladies of the congregation, a practice of mine upon the high holidays. Yet my eyes were at once drawn to this small silent figure, and, as I passed, her dark eyes looked up at me for a moment shining with the ethereality of innocence, illuminating her pale unpainted face and her lips full and bright with young blood. I at once decided, in that crowd of easily available wives and mistresses of the horned horde of Venetian husbands, to ignore rich luxuries eager to be tasted, for only this little nun would satisfy my palate.

So that day in Lent, as the service choralled to its end, I knelt willing my little bride of Christ to thoughts of adultery. Impatient for her as I was then, I used my new-found magic to speed me through the tricks and pretences, the investigations, the bribery and persuasion that led me, some weeks later, to a consummation, in the summer-house of the palazzo of a nobleman whose gardens adjoined those of the convent of the Order which had failed to protect its little sister of mercy from my irresistible lust. All this was the more enjoyable a second time, for now I brought with me the perceptions of an elder connoisseur of the sex, and that hunger of the ageing lecher which is not so quickly satisfied as the eager appetites of a young man. But what was this? As I mouthed my little quarry delicately, what was it I perceived from the vantage of my experience that I had not seen before? Was it an inconsiderable but definite crook to the eyes, a slight pendulousness of a damp lower lip, a doubtfulness in her protests more suited to a subtle whore than a daughter of God? I could not be certain, but some voice whispered through the endless beds searched since that time for extraordinary tidbits, advising me that things were not entirely as they appeared. Speeding my time-carriage onwards, I quickly passed through many devices to discover what I had not found out at the time of my eager enjoyment of the creature, that she was daughter to a ducal family which had for centuries bestowed upon its scions twin heritages of great wealth and corruption, which latter, in Teresa's case, emerged as a taste for being despoiled in a nun's habit. So disappointed, so profoundly hurt was I to discover that this innocence which my soul craved was a mere simulation, that I felt sick. I recollected that in my former experience of this adventure, protected by my unawareness, I had enjoyed the seduction immensely and innocently through weeks of subtle and amusing invention. But now, having seen the truth, I no longer had the ability to re-experience my former happiness; now, infuriated by her deceptions, I deserted my little Carmelite Duchess, and hurried away in a paroxysm of hatred before my heart could suffer more bruises.

Speedily I flicked through other enjoyable experiences of that time, often remembered as a most successful year of my mid-life, and selected adventures more creditable than the simulated cries of joy of the whorish little daughter of Lilith. And so, eventually, I proceeded to the casino to relive a particular night of astounding luck at the tables. I remembered that I had left there in the fresh early hours of the morning to saunter through the herb-market, my pockets heavy with gold and several attractive trifles of jewellery. The casino, as I now re-entered its doors, had more the quality of a low gambling house than the elegant brightness I remembered. I shrugged and noted, frowning with displeasure, that the ladies of the house were over-painted, and that if one ventured too close to them, one perceived ugly spots upon their cheeks, revealed as sweat melted the pink and white chemical blanket concealing them. I noted, too, a strong eructation of evil breath which, in the nights of my halcyon days, seemed never to bother me. And, withal, there was an excitement missing, my pulse did not race, and, yawning, I thought longingly of my bed. Nevertheless, the game was running high when I joined it. I accepted my cards and, without looking at them, threw several gold coins upon the table. Tired, bloodshot eyes looked at me suspiciously from above their own cards as my opponents laid their bets. Still unconcerned with what I had been dealt, I raised my stake, to a murmur of incredulity and a few scattered curses. Now flicking my cards over with one hand, I reached for the stakes with the other, for I remembered well from the past this particular *grand coup*. But my confidence was mistaken by the other players to be a sure indication that I had committed some extraordinary subtlety upon the cards, and that I was, to put it simply, a common cheat. I found my winnings retained by several hands, and, when I pro-

tested, was greeted with suggestions that I prove
my good fortune with my sword.

None of this, I need hardly remark, was as I
remembered it, for it seemed that a victory re-
visited loses its original virtue; and now the story
was bruited about the city that Casanova had been
caught cheating (a distinct possibility in other circumstances, but quite untrue in this particular
instance), and, my honour impugned, my credit
rapidly disappeared. Several husbands now tacitly
agreed that I would be more comfortable floating
face-downwards in a lagoon, and, in the early hours
of the mornings attempts were made upon my life
by brutal ruffians. Though I successfully defended
myself with my second-best Toledo blade, I could
not discourage the horned gentlemen of Venice

from lodging complaints against me on the grounds of my being a notorious magician. Short of cash, I determined to leave the ungrateful city of foetid canals, financing my departure by selling some forged manuals of magic to an eager buyer who turned out to be a government spy. I have already elegantly and feelingly described what followed in my Memoirs, but here I was transported yet again to that dreadful prison in the roof of the Doge's Palace, the infamous Leads, for, although nothing was precisely as it had been, suddenly all was now as it had concluded. To resolve any confusion about the strange experience, let me explain simply that I had indeed been transported to an earlier time, which turned out to be not nearly as enjoyable as I remembered it, containing elements which I appeared to have forgotten or eliminated when committing them to my Memoirs. Sensing that the unpleasantness of incarceration in the Leads was unlikely to be much relieved in this second living of it, I made a great leap of my will and at once found myself cold and stiff, my head between my knees, in Stichka's kitchen, confronted by the congealed carcase of a roast porker and the relaxed figure of an old Jew reading by candlelight in a corner of the smoking fireplace.

The Jew smiled at me as if pleased to have my company again. 'So you have decided to return,' he observed.

'A pox upon your magic,' I groaned, raising myself painfully.

60

'I warned you, did I not, that going backwards with a mature understanding of reality prejudices one's pleasures, though I see that you are returned safely, little affected by your experience.'

'Little affected?' I exclaimed, searching for the brandy bottle. 'Here you have taken the joy from my most joyous memories with your accursed tricks of time-travel, and how shall I ever be the same again? How, indeed, shall I finish my Memoirs without the delusions which made the living of them so pleasant?'

'You will not finish your Memoirs,' the old man prophesied confidently, 'but through the volumes you have written up to your forty-ninth year, you will enjoy a considerable post-mortem success, bringing to your name an immortality which none of the transports of your life would have merited without your elegant descriptions. That must be some comfort to you.'

'Comfort! Is it a comfort to be told that fools will enjoy one's life when one is no longer able to enjoy it oneself? A multiple pox upon my future readers and an agonizing death to the scoundrelly publishers who will get fat dining upon my dead bones! A curse upon all living follies! Must I return to a life of pissed-upon polenta? Never! I will not do it! I will die first!'

The old fellow stared at me solemnly for a moment, nodding slowly. 'An excellent idea,' he said. 'What method of despatch would you favour?'

(III)

The old man stared challengingly
at me for a minute

OH, THE TRICKERY of these Jews! Can an honest Christian ever outwit them? Oh, the arrogance of this elderly Semitic artisan standing before one of my rank, one who learnt his catechism at the very feet of the Pope! When I was a younger man, the fire of my temperament would have been kindled by this Kabbalistic capering. My sword would have been at his throat in a trice, and the Jew-dog would know once and for all what it was to approach the splendour of the throne upon the chariot of his four-lettered God. I have never been entirely comfortable in the presence of Jews, although these latter years in dirty Duchkov have made me, if not more tolerant, then certainly less discriminating. I remember only one good Jew with whom I was forced to share a carriage, and who turned out to be a truly fine-natured and simple-minded fellow. He produced the most excellent pâté I have ever eaten. It was made by his daughter from a secret recipe of the Jews in which something extraordinary is perpetrated upon the livers of chickens. I subsequently lodged with him, seduced his daughter, introduced her to the forbidden delicacy of oysters and generally supplemented her restricted Jew-education. But now there was no pâté and no daughter, just this impertinent and incompetent Kabbalistic cobbler confronting me, and, with the arrogant certainty of his people, daring to postulate my surcease. I calmed myself and studied the ancient dotard contemptuously. 'I would guess, Jew,' I said, my own man again, 'that you yourself are nearer to eighty years of age than I am myself, although I concede that you appear to be in excellent condition. Nevertheless, of us two, I am the younger man and should still have something to expect from life. In which case, sir, the question arises why should you not precede me? In short, sir, if you are so keen on suicide, why the Devil do you not commit it yourself? This friendly agreement you offer me on my own surcease is damnably annoying, considering you have already trifled with my memories. Have you no comfort for me? Have you no means of persuading me to remain among the living? Cannot you offer the smallest hope to a troubled fellow-being?'

The strange shoe-maker stood up, stretched, sighed, put down his book and seated himself beside me. 'Do not consider, sir,' he said gently, 'that I discriminate especially in your favour in the matter of suicide. In my endless travels among our species, I have frequently observed that a large number of our fellows would be better off dead and the rest of us less harmed by their being so. For not everything in creation that has the potential of life is required to follow that course. Nature creates in profusion because she understands very well that the greater part of life is wastage; from a million

66

seeds one oak may grow. From an hundred thousand tadpoles one frog may survive. Why, then , do we expect her to value our own species more highly? No sir; it is clear to me that human life is as much superfluous to the best intentions of our common mother as are the rest of her children. Why, after all, should she discriminate in our favour, even though we pray to a God we have surmised in order to give us a pre-eminence we cannot otherwise prove? And, surely, sir, when a frog has enjoyed as much eating, drinking, learning, folly, cheating, hoping and despairing as the Chevalier de Seingalt, and if there is now little more left to him than despair, sickness, complaints and loose teeth, then surely, sir, what remains of his Reason must calmly beckon him towards Death?'

One does not spend a night corroding one's interior with violent liquor in a kitchen redolent of cold roast pork, with no company other than an itinerant Jew-cobbler, in order to be told that one would be better off speeding the inevitable journey towards the abyss. Such cold comfort Job may seek; but this idiotic patience with the obscure and dreadful intentions of the Almighty and His consort Nature is not consonant with my character.

'And what about your own eating, drinking, folly, despair and bad teeth?' I replied angrily, though as far as I could see, this fellow had a mouthful of strong, yellowing teeth which, amazingly, seemed to be his own. 'I take it,' I continued, 'that copulation is certainly no more frequent an experience for you these days than it is for myself. Incidentally, where did you have your teeth made?' I helped myself to some crackling from the left hind quarter of the pig and crunched it noisily.

'They are my own,' the stranger replied. 'My family was always blessed with good teeth and excellent health, but in your other surmise you are correct, sir. I lost interest in copulatory matters and other illusions of the flesh many years ago. For it eventually occurred to me that there was little point and no dignity whatsoever in making a great fuss about an activity in which any dog may engage.'

Feeling there was some concealed insult to my public reputation in this remark, I immediately insisted, 'There is no comparison whatsoever between what you so charmlessly call the copulatory matters of dog and Man.' I tore off another piece of crackling from the carcase, suddenly savagely hungry.

'That is true,' he replied, nodding his head sagely, 'for the canine species has only a limited number of days of heat each month, whereas unfortunate Man is the victim of his instinct both day and night the whole month through. I am constantly revolving this matter,' he mused to himself, 'endeavouring to understand why. For in Nature there appears to be some reason in everything, yet in Man's continuous and ennervating preoccupation with the hind quarters of his sexual partners there seems to be no sense whatsoever. Kabbalah suggests that we strive for a union symbolical of the marriage of Torah and Shekinah. It may be so, but I seriously doubt it.'

'Why, my dear fellow!' I exclaimed, delighted to become mentor for once to the tedious sage, 'the solution to your problem is immediately clear to me. Consider, of all creatures Man is the only one who plays games, and the pursuit of the fair sex is the greatest game of all. It is the most dangerous gamble, offering the most unexpected consequences of loss and gain. For often when one gains, one has won nothing but trouble, unquiet and disease; and when one loses, one has gained a delightful, if occasionally boring, interlude of peace. The pursuit of love demonstrates more than any other human game the impossibility of assessing the value of wining or losing in life. *Vive l'amour!*'

'It is a drug, sir.'

'Of course, it is! For when we see a hue of the eyes, a tone of the skin, a line of limb, that reminds us of our earliest satisfactions and joys, some part of our minds, some organ of the brain is stimulated to respond, and we follow instantly, for the fulfilment of this response is unalloyed pleasure. And, as with all intense pleasures, we become addicted to it, as I am proud and happy to have been from my earliest days. To Eros I have given my heart and soul in worship! *Ave* Eros!'

'*Ave atque vale,*' my cobbler-philosopher replied. 'But I see that your eyes sparkle, signor, your lips grow moist and full, your nostrils sniffing at the air

69

like a stallion charging into the fray. Clearly you, yet again, in spite of your recent time-ride, have the illusion that you are twenty-five and fit for anything. I put it to you, sir, that this folly demonstrates conclusively you are not yet ready to make your quietus.' He sighed deeply. 'I regret this, for as the divine Dante has observed, "It is a comfort to those who dwell in misery to have companionship."'

I frowned. 'Let me understand you aright,' I said. 'Do you yourself entertain some night-thoughts of *felo da se*?'

'I would the termination of my follies were so simply won!' He breathed a profound and age-old sigh.

'Ah!' I exclaimed, 'then you too, in spite of your

Kabbalah and time-travelling, hesitate at the edge of the grimpen?'

'Hear me, my friend,' the Jew replied sadly, (for men who have discussed love and death together must be considered friends), 'would you believe it if I confessed that I have on numerous occasions opened my arms wide to the Great Ravisher, and that she refuses the offer of my embrace?'

'How well-expressed!' I said. 'The embrace of the Ravisher, indeed. And she refuses your offer? Suddenly, sir, I seem to understand the whole matter. Approaching Death is just another game of seduction. I thank you for the thought, sir, and trust you will not be put out if I say that, while you have been often refused, I, sir, cannot remember an unsuccessful conclusion to a seductive gambit. I am the master-player of that game. If I court Death, believe me, she will finish in my arms.'

'Certainly you will in hers,' he responded kindly. 'Do you, I wonder, have an especial approach in mind? Are you inclined to the Roman style, to fall forward upon your sword or open your wrists in a warm bath? Perhaps you have studied the secrets of berries that darken at night and of sickly spotted mushrooms? Perhaps you cunningly plot to use the offices of an enemy in a contrived duel? I tell you freely, my friend, here in the lengthening shadows of Eros and Thanatos, I have tried all these and many more, and live on to tell the tale.'

'Well, sir Jew,' I replied, sniffing the air as if his failure stank, 'reduced in means as I am, my magic

71

is more reliable than yours, for I do not lack the power to command Death.'

'I believe you,' the old man replied simply. 'It would be yet another indication of Nature's strange balance that you who have fathered so many unknowns should have a special relationship with the greatest unknown of all.'

I jabbed my hand under his long nose. 'Smell here, this bloodstone on which is engraved the arms of my title, Chevalier de Seingalt, granted to me by the common consent of the nobility of the Netherlands.'

'An impressive escutcheon,' the old man said. 'How does it speak to Death?'

'Behind this proud design,' I explained, 'there is concealed a potent mixture of lethal herbs, the recipe of the last Great Witch of Muran. Cast into the foulest wine, it will not only improve the flavour, but transform it to a deathly potion.' I sprang a minute lever, and the bloodstone opened to reveal a piece of folded gold foil within which the deathly gift awaited release.

'Is there sufficient for two?' the old man asked, his bushy eyebrows raised.

'For twenty. There is release in every grain.' I sighed deeply. 'I have kept this powder long concealed in my ring; ever since I escaped from the Leads and thought it might be wise to carry upon my person a certain exit from any prison. I often thought of using it profitably upon someone else, but enacting in my mind some future triumphant escape from evil captors, I preserved it, though never truly believing that I was saving it for myself.'

'If your potion has the power for which you praise it, I would be most curious to try it,' the old man replied.

'Well, so be it,' I replied, somewhat surprised. 'Although I cannot recommend the wine here for one's last taste of life.' I held up a two-thirds empty wine-bottle to the light of the spitting candle upon the table. It was an appalling colour. I sniffed at it. It yielded up the vinegar smell of the sour dregs of my life. 'It is not good enough for our enjoyment,' I observed to my companion, offering him the bottle, 'but perfectly suited to drinking to such institutions as the House of Wallenstein and Death.'

With what might perhaps have been considered a slightly operatic gesture, I waved my hand over a pewter cup which the old man had selected as our chalice and filled it with noxious wine, releasing the Witch of Muran's secret into it. The old man stared challengingly at me for a minute and then solemnly offered the cup. I was about to take it when it occurred to me that it would be appallingly bad manners to depart this world without leaving a charming note of thanks to my host. 'A moment,' I requested, 'while I scribble an extremely short letter (well-suited to publication) to Lord Waldstein.' I searched my pockets for a fragment of clean paper. 'Would you believe,' I mused, 'that this Fauchenkircher expects me to pay for the paper I use for my Memoirs? In spite of the fact that

I am dedicating the work to our Lord of Dux. Do you realize how expensive good paper is? I find it sensuously most unpleasant to write upon poor quality paper.'

I fished a handful of crumpled, tattered documents from my inside pocket and glanced at them. Laundry bills. Two hotel bills from years ago. Was this all there was left of a long half-century of determined posturing? How right I was to kill myself. 'But look here. Look at this absurdity.' I offered a yellowing note to the old man. 'A list of items of clothing headed "What I must wear at Dresden". What would you say to such a posturing coxcomb? And what's this?' I looked at another note to myself from the past, '"Reflections on Respiration and the True Cause of Health", medical discoveries of mine to which I owe my present excellent condition, no doubt. Pompous charlatan! And here, mysteriously, just two words: "the crows". A prophecy perhaps of the two of us, two tattered companions of the shades, trying to fly still. I must say, it is quite fascinating to look through one's old papers. Oh, my genius! Look at this: "A new method for winning the lottery at Rome". I lost. And here. An important document for crossing the Styx: "Passport pour Monsieur de Casanova, Venetian alland d'ici en Holland, Octobre 13, 1738. Ce passport bon pour quinze jours". I was returning to my little Dutch lady Marietta. She was obsessed with my cabal. "Tell me your secret, Monsieur Casanova," she begged, "and you may command of me whatsoever your

74

heart desires." My cabal was a little numerological trick for making prophecies, a total cheat of course, but my desires were genuine. Goodbye, little witch Marietta. Let me remember your delights as I drift on the wind, an old crow, floating away from disgusting Duchkov. Now in one draught!' I accepted the cup from the damnably persistent old hand which produced it now from the limbo of the table.

'Leave some for me, good friend,' the old man requested with what seemed to be a somewhat ironic smile.

'You are my guest in disgusting Duchkov and should drink first,' I insisted, repelling the cup towards him politely. Surely his offer to join me in my last adventure was a mere *politesse?*

'You are always generous, Seigneur.' The stranger coughed, a short, high-pitched, giggling cough which sounded most unpleasant, like the snickering of a midget demon. Lifting the cup slowly, he quaffed what must have been half its contents in one swallow. I watched him, amazed, appalled, quite horrified. His action, compelling as a challenge to a duel, had deprived me of freedom to do anything now other than drain the cup and glimpse the toad in its lees! So would die the gallant Chevalier, Knight of the Papal Order of the Gold Spur. I should be wearing my decorations at such a moment. I searched for the Gold Spur only the other day, but without success. Could that apple-cheeked little minx have taken it? I should have given her a little present perhaps.

The old man was pointing the lethal cup forward towards my heart. He raised it to my lips. The bitter liquor touched them. I swallowed a little. Oh, bitter, bitter! Then, 'One moment, friend,' I gabbled nervously, taking the cup gingerly from him. 'It is all very well for a cobbler to proceed directly to the pit, but I am an author, and I must scribble my farewell to life. The ingenious travelling desk given to me by an intellectual Polish Princess (a unique phenomenon in Poland) is with my luggage in the other room, if you will excuse me, sir, for a moment.'

I bowed and left quickly, the old fool reassuring me, 'I have left you a full half of the potion.' Appalling wretch! Why could not he have drunk the lot? There was still enough left for a small cavalry detachment, including the horses. I spat out venomously, but the acid taste still haunted my tongue.

In the adjoining room I retrieved my charming miniature *écritoire*, and, having done so, settled down in the cool, stale air to compose a suitable curtain speech. With a fresh quill, I wrote upon the back of the fine quality folio sheet of my ancient passport the following words:

> Short reflection of a philosopher who finds himself procuring his escape from: being kept awake by dogs, disablement to his digestion by polluted polenta, the craven impudence of grubby servants, the ingratitude of former benefactors greatly benefited by his efforts, etcetera, etcetera, etcetera. 13 October, 1797; day dedicated to Saint Lucy and memorable as the last of my too-long life.

I must recall a few pungent phrases.

> All fools are not proud, but all proud men are fools.
> Many fools are happy, all proud men are unhappy.

Frederick II stole that from me. Well, why not? It is quite meaningless. I shall write without pretension, thus:

> Life is a burden to me. Reason convinces me that the power I have of slaying myself is a privilege given to me by what God there may be. *Qui non potest vivere bene non vivat male.* He who cannot live well should not live badly. I thank you, Count von Waldstein, for your hospitality

which could have been both better and worse. You may sell my few miserable possessions to repay any small sums outstanding to yourself and your excellent servants. Casanova bids you, the world, and the lovely flesh, farewell.

I read the note over aloud. I liked the simple dignity of it very much indeed. 'Casanova bids you farewell,' I repeated, and emptied the pewter cup over the smouldering embers of the fireplace. They smoked and steamed, putting out a low purple noxious flame and a loathsome stench.

I collapsed into a deep wainscot chair totally exhausted by my ordeal. As the filthy smell of the poison assaulted my nostrils, I sweated to think how near I had ventured to Death, yet had I conquered her. For it was clear to me by the time I finished composing my eloquent note, that it is the height of folly to speed oneself towards a dreary and inevitable last assignation, particularly since, like my Jew, I have always entertained the gravest doubts about the world to come, failing to see how it can be at all gallant whilst accommodating so many. Imagine, countless millions of completely uninteresting, ugly, good, plain souls crowding one's progress in every direction! For my part I have never been one to lose my identity in a large crowd. So, if Heaven exists, it is no place for an uncontrite and un-confessed Jacques Casanova; imagine the frustration of meeting again those hundreds of pretty souls whose bodies I have enjoyed, there being no present means of reachieving pleasure together! And then the absence of good wine, piquant sauces and delicately flavoured fruits of the sea! Without such simple but essential joys, how, I wonder, may they call it Heaven?

I felt my pulse. My heartbeat was now more regular. The room felt suddenly cold and my best silk shirt, wet with my sweat, seemed an icy shroud. I shivered, but even as I did so, laughed to myself to think how the old Cavalier had once again escaped incarceration, this time in a jail from which even he could never have escaped. I tossed my farewell note upon the embers and, having watched it flare up and burn brightly, decided to return to the kitchen to see how the unexpectedly impetuous old cobbler had fared. I was most curious to discover whether my poison had preserved its deathly powers, or whether the years had rendered it harmless. But as I stood there, a sudden rending pain assaulted the general area of my intestines. I thought at once that the poison was killing me; then remembered I had not taken it. The foul brandy, perhaps. And then the waves of agony were lifted by a massive gust of wind which, breaking out as a gigantic and most unusually elongated fart, informed me that fear of the imminence of Death had blessed my bowels, a benison often prayed for these past several weeks when they were so stubbornly inactive that I had thought my fundament blocked for ever. Now it seemed that, instead of dying that night, I would achieve what is, for the old, almost as great a pleasure as the evacuations of love are for the

79

young. I hurried on my comfortable, well-shod feet towards the disgusting common jakes which, in my present circumstances, seemed a veritable Shrine of Cloacina. Totally forgetful of all my troubles, I hastened with short steps, each one encouraged by a loud petard, a braying trumpet urging the brave warrior to the field of battle.

(IV)

*What a piece of work is
Man's bowels*

WHAT A PIECE OF WORK is Man's bowels! As I
sat upon the worn wooden seat overhanging a
blessedly deep pit (for the jakes of a tavern is
appallingly over-used), I thought as I often had
before when engaged in my business, how this
astounding mechanism of one's intestinal machine
works day after day, if one is healthy, young and
blessed, or even when cursed by the tardiness of
old age, at least every week or so, for it was
certainly a week or more, perhaps even two weeks,
since I had made so successful a delivery. I had on
several nights lately crept, holding a candle before
me, along the cold corridors of Duchkov to the
nearest cloaca, some half-mile away, my feet
frozen, my stomach griping, a foul taste in my
mouth, but a growing sense of urgency speeding
me on, to come to rest, grunting and breathing
heavily, upon the ice-cold stone seat overhanging
the turrets of the castle walls with a direct trajectory
into the moat. The wind blew up one's anus, the
pangs receded, yet one was lucky to reply with
the smallest eructation. So, sit and read some
small volume of gallant adventures for an hour or
so, straining every five minutes to see if the per-
verse sphincter had changed its mind, the lower

83

intestine having decided to behave like a good Christian and be blessed in its giving. Still nothing but the odd miserable little squealing complaint, more suited to one of His Lordship's cretinous babes, no relief at all.

Of course, it is the servants and their continuous pilfering. Whenever he is in residence, His Lordship has fresh butter on his fresh polenta, green olive oil in his salad dressing, the best of flesh and fowl; and so he imagines that the culinary condition of Duchkov is as the housekeeping accounts suggest, with excellent materials crudened in the cuisine. Waldstein enjoys tastelessly, greedy, no gourmet, but even he and his oafish friends will eventually notice if the fish is off, the oil stale, or the meat too high. But while the Teutonic dwarfs stuffed their gross paunches, I, the only true intellectual in Bohemia, must offer to my delicate stomach all year round, dinnertime after dinnertime, the poorest of viands, old rancid oil and stale fish. In such circumstances how could one expect the miracle of regular balanced action from one's bowels? Yet here in this stinking tavern jakes a miracle occurred, a spectacular and most enjoyable delivery. I recollected, as I hoisted my riding breeches afterwards, how, on one or two occasions in my long life I had experienced fear, and it had most urgently loosened my bowels. In the past I had not the courage to admit it easily but now I did so, blessing the devious and subtle ways of Nature by which I had profited. Yet my mouth still felt a little contracted from the bitterness of the potion.

Could it be, I wondered, that the liquid taken *in parvo* had hastened the revolution of my innards?

Whatever it was, feeling several years younger, flatter in the stomach, and somewhat lighter in weight, I returned thoughtfully to the kitchen intending, if the old man who had been the unwitting agent of my relief were still alive, to thank him. But, oh, horror! As I entered, I saw that my strange benefactor was collapsed in the abandoned posture of one who has died with sudden agonizing violence. He was slumped on the bench where we had sat together talking philosophy, his head awkwardly thrown back, his face away from me, his long legs stuck forward stiffly as if the arctic climate of Death had already ascended from his feet upwards. Horrified as I was to see how narrowly I had yet again escaped (for clearly the Murano poison had not lost its pristine potency), I could not but feel a small pang of regret for the demise of this odd fellow for there was, I discovered by consulting my watch (the gift of a French Princess), still three hours to wait before the arrival of the post-chaise, and time hangs heavy when there is no one with whom to make amusing conversation.

As I completed the adjustment of my dress in the comfort of the fire's warmth, I ruminated sadly upon the inadequacy of Man that, no matter how brilliant he may be, conversation with himself tends to pall after a while. He needs the company of others as audience to confirm his laughter and his tears. How I had missed the plays of the glittering world since my incarceration in Bohemia with its vulgar kitchen comedies! How I remember the pleasures of my box in the Teatro la Fenice in Venice; the delight of the dangers of discovery; the rosy blushes warming delicate cheeks as buttons were surreptitiously adjusted and flounces replaced to conceal the startling surprise of exposed thighs as the curtain rose upon the second act. The last button of my breeches came off in my fingers, and I flicked it onto the embers in the fireplace and recollected that I was presently involved in a tragedy of real life, alone in the middle of the night with a haunch of roast pork and a dead man for company. I sighed considering the unexpected turns of life, asking myself (as I had so often in the past) whether strength of character may be successfully opposed to the generally irresistible forces of Destiny. I believe so for my instinct for life being strong, why, here I stood warming my ice-cold backside in the fireplace, while he who, according to his own account, had scotched Death so often in the past, was now her eternal companion.

Then it came to me as many of the greatest ideas do, in the most unexpected of circumstances. It occurred to me that a weaker dose of my Murano potion, appealingly packaged, might make me a fortune; for many are afflicted by constipation, the striving against which produces those painful engorgements which protrude from the rectum like giant grapes and are responsible for much of the savagery of Man towards his brother. Common piles and constipation persecute all men from the

86

commonest to the highest, the stupidest and those of genius, often being responsible for the sharpness of the latters' wit. Take M. Voltaire for example. I visited him in Ferney and found him a rude and self-opinionated bore who considered himself an immortal, even while he frowned and grimaced, searching with his bony backside for a position to relieve the pressure on his quite mortal piles. He had the audacity to tell me that my excellent translations of Horace were bad. That great rationalist, the eternal enemy of superstition, cant and religiosity, how I laughed when he died some years ago! For he who spat out the Bible, rightly ridiculing its dogmas, was not ashamed at the extremity of his life to beg for the sacraments. He covered his body with more relics than the so-called Saint Louis at Amboise, an unregenerate sinner who was serviced by ladies till the very moment of his death. Sensible enough arrangement, but the Devil protect me from such a recantation when my time comes, as it almost had so recently. Yet instead, my instinct for life triumphed again; Death had kissed my lips briefly and left upon them the bitter taste of Casanova's Soothe for Enflamed Entrails. A little honey will improve the flavour of poppy, mandragora and other secrets. I have the formula written down somewhere and will search it out later for I do believe there is a fortune in it. 'Thanks again, good old Jew,' I said, for my Jew was dead and therefore entirely good, but then my heart leapt, and I jumped several inches in the air with shock, for the outspread body of the cobbler moved!

Being in no hurry to investigate the fellow's condition, I reminded myself that fresh corpses have a tendency to jerk and stretch as the stiffening process overwhelms them. But there had been about the old Jew, from the first moment of our encounter, a quality of strangeness, a certain grandeur even, an occasional tone of authority which suggested that here was no simple mortal, but one whom arcane knowledge and rare experience had made exceptional. For though I have long ago discovered that there are no unseen forces that play hide and seek with one another using our bodies and minds for concealment, yet I do believe that there are among us those rare ones who, like myself, have exceptional character, genius and talent, and that members of this élite seem often by their powers of mind and spirit to be superhuman. I had recognized that the cobbler was one of us few; my instant intimacy with him proved him exceptional, for I am not one to make friends and suicide pacts so quickly. But no matter how extraordinary my old new friend might have been, I knew there was no way in which he could conquer a large dose of the potion of Muran (if it were still lethal). At which point in my musings, the body heaved itself upright on the bench as one might after an exceptionally profound sleep. Turning its visage toward me, it addressed me thus: 'So Casanova,' the corpse said, 'either we are dead and Paradise or Hell is a dirty kitchen smelling of roast pork, or your poison is no more practical than your old man's lust.'

The Jew slowly stood up. He advanced towards me. I backed away, still uncertain as to the status of the fellow. 'There is also,' he observed, continuing to march, 'another possibility. That you, my friend, are as accursed as I. Tell the truth, Casanova, does not Death spurn you?'

I felt my eyes expand unnaturally in their sockets as I stared at him. 'Speak!' the Jew intoned. 'Tell me your secret, gallant Chevalier, and I will tell you mine.'

But my tongue clove to the roof of my mouth; for, as the flickering light of the candle on the table illuminated his features, I was appalled to observe myself confronted not by the aged man of eighty years or so whom I had taken for dead, but by a clear-eyed and energetic young beardless fellow of some thirty years, erect with vitality, the fire of life

bright in his eyes. My back now as close to the fireplace as it might come without the satin of my breeches burning, the stranger advanced his head close to mine and enquired in a hoarse whisper: 'Tell me, Casanova, art thou immortal as I?'

'Immortal?' I mumbled stupidly, for I had still not absorbed the shock of his appearance; yet I pulled myself together and responded quickly enough. 'Would I permit myself to be a seventy-year-old librarian in Duchkov if I were immortal? Immortal!' I laughed harshly. I held the fellow back, noting that he was substantial enough and therefore of this world. 'But you, sir, will you explain yourself?' Is it, I suddenly wondered, my witch's brew that has restored his youth? Oh, how my labouring heart sank in my breast! Had I possessed in my ring all these painful years without knowing it, the Elixir of Life? And, *horribile dictu*! had I thrown upon the embers my only chance to escape old age? But what stupid questions I am asking myself, my mind responded. Had I not sold the spurious hope of eternal youth half-a-dozen times in my career? Did I not know of a certainty that no one can effect a transformation from apparent age to actual youth without trickery? And so I rapidly concluded that my former old bearded cobbler was this same young fellow with the beard removed and the greasepaint lines rubbed from his face. 'Come, sir, what is the purpose of this trick?' I repeated my question sternly, whereupon tears spouted from the young man's eyes, and he wept like a heartbroken child.

90

'Come, come, sir, don't be so distressed. We must be manly when our tricks go awry. Yours has done no harm, and indeed, I am grateful to you for it, for though you have startled me, you have also relieved me of a heavy burden of guilt, were I one to entertain such feelings. Here, sir,' I handed him the lace handkerchief from my sleeve. 'Dry your eyes and let us sit down and explain to me the purpose of this deception. For I have always been a serious student of such trickery and have on no few occasions practised it to my own great profit and amusement. So come, my surprisingly young friend, sit down, drink a little of this appalling brandy and tell me what you hoped to gain by your apparent death followed by this amazing apparent transformation. For I will admit that I did take you entirely for my senior in age; and now I am still a little amazed to discover that you are in reality a young man.'

The stranger returned my damp kerchief to me. 'Alas,' he said sadly. 'I had high hopes for your potion.'

'Ah, well,' I comforted him, 'it had remained unused too long and, like all who save themselves excessively, lost its potency. But relieve my curiosity, sir. Confirm my judgement. You were engaged in some trick of confidence, the object of which I have not as yet discerned? Is that not so?'

My new young man regarded me with great intensity. 'I swear to you, Signor, it was my most earnest hope that your potion would prove to be my quietus. I long to die,' he continued, a strange thrilling note in his voice. 'It is my dream and hope,

91

my only ambition. As I waited here for your poison to work to its happy conclusion, I blessed you with all my heart. But no, it was not to be. It will never be. I must continue without rest to wander the world, for ever waiting.'

Tears welled up again in his eyes and ran down his cheeks, but I did not offer him my kerchief again. It seemed to me that this fellow cried altogether too easily. Beginning to lose my patience, I replied irritably, 'Well, sir, pull yourself together and answer my question. What the Devil did you hope to gain by simulating an ancient cobbler? Your most convincing performance has, as far as I can see, achieved only two ends, neither of which is profitable to yourself. Though I am most grateful to have my boots repaired and my bowels vacant, what profit, I repeat, does this pantomime bring to you?'

He sipped brandy from his glass moodily and was silent.

'Well, sir,' I reminded him severely, 'I await your answer.'

'Signor Casanova,' he replied eventually, looking at me most earnestly, 'it is not my practice to tell my story to many for it often evokes fear, loathing and hatred. But I know you to be a man of Reason, and believe therefore that you will be able to bring both credence and sensible comprehension to my tale. But, sir,' he continued, 'cut me, if you will, a slice or two of pork, for this process of dying and being reborn gives one a most unholy appetite, and I shall need all my strength to tell you my story.'

I was, to tell the truth, feeling somewhat empty myself and was not at all unpleased to join this odd young fellow in a middle-of-the-night breakfast. I often in the library saved myself some bread and goat-cheese, and, dull and dry as it became stored behind Dante, I much enjoyed the nocturnal picnic it provided, tossing crumbs to the curious mice who looked up at me in surprised gratitude. So I carved us meat, and found bread, radishes, a raw onion and some wilting leaves of lettuce. 'But I fear there is no oil, vinegar or herbs to make my special dressing,' I apologized. My companion fell upon the meat and bread as if he had not eaten for a week. Watching him, I lost my own appetite for anything other than the tale he had promised to tell me. I knew as an old teller of tales myself that it would be a good one.

'I am,' the fellow said, through a mouthful of pork, 'the Wandering Jew.' He raised a large thick

piece of crackling to his lips where his excellent teeth received it, masticating it as efficiently as a cat crunches a black beetle.

Startled for a moment, I soon was helpless with laughter. He stared at me continuing to eat ravenously. Eventually, as he lifted a thick pink slice of meat to his mouth, I managed to gasp out, 'Jews, my poor charlatan, do not eat pork!' whereupon I again collapsed, laughing at the fellow's careless effrontery.

Eventually, wheezing noisily, but still enjoying the joke, I looked at the false Jew, my cheeks wet with tears, and awaited his response.

'You are perfectly right in your observation,' he replied eventually through a full mouth. 'But while Jews do not eat pork, as is well-known, you surely will not deny that they could eat it if they would. And then you must take into consideration the many Jews who have been forced into baptism. They often have their sincerity tested by a porcine morsel, and yield to it. Then again, there are those who are and would remain Jews, but seek some protective behaviour. What could serve them better than an occasional slice of bacon? I could continue quoting such examples, but I would be surprised if as rational a Christian as yourself would require me to. I would, however, put it to you as a subject worthy of your consideration, that many who have been taken for Jews have not been so. And they, of course, would, in the natural flow of events, eat pork.'

'You would not,' I, somewhat put out, asked the

impertinent fellow, 'care to enlarge upon your having become at least thirty years younger since our last meeting? I will tell you frankly that it is my own conclusion that you have, throughout our acquaintance, actually been of your present age and have simulated an older man than myself by the skilful use of false hair, a little paint and an admittedly imposing manner. I remember once in Prague I used similiar devices to convince my prey, a wealthy but extremely greedy glass-merchant, that I possessed the secret formulas which ensure eternal life. Early observations of my parents (my father being an actor and my mother a highly sought-after but somewhat inconsistent opera-singer, neither of whom had much time for the dull child I then was), taught me that false hair and a little cosmetic colour expertly used, easily dupe anyone eager to be fooled. In Prague I enjoyed, as a result of my own successful deception, a substantial part of the glass-merchant's wealth together with excellent lodgings for some six months or so, and the favours of his wife (eager also to find youth wherever she could), his daughter, (desperately in need of a civilized education after the barbarisms of the Bohemian capital) and two housemaids who, while not having the gift of restoring youth to their master, had certainly helped to age him. As for this trick of the eternal Jew, I am familiar with it. There are several pamphlets on the subject in my library. They appeared under the imprint of Christoff Creutzer, Leyden, 1602. My memory for such bibliographic details is amazing; indeed my

95

memory altogether is remarkable. There are several other such pamphlets published during the next decade. The author, an otherwise unknown hand named therein as Chrysostom Dudulaeus Westphalus, clearly a pseudonym, perhaps originating from the word "Dudler" meaning one who mumbles; but do not let us get lost in these bibliographic details. I was amused to find these items and identified and catalogued them recollecting my own experience some years ago as a "Wandering Jew".'

I watched my companion keenly. He wiped his mouth but made no other response to my revelation.

'Are you not surprised to hear that I, too, have been he whom you simulated?' I insisted.

He picked his perfect teeth as he replied, 'There are many imposters. There have been many, there are several about presently, and there will be more to come.' He reached for an apple.

'These publications,' I continued, 'describe our subject as very tall with long hair, bare of foot, with strangely thick skin on his feet –'

The stranger laughed shortly and bitterly. 'An idiocy of the peasant mind that retails these stories,' he commented. 'Naturally having walked for eighteen centuries, one's feet would have developed thick skin like that of an elephant. The stupid literalness of the human mind!'

I agreed. 'Nevertheless, according to these sources, the gentleman in question spent a good deal of time in church, beating his breast and sighing deeply. He, too, was a shoe-maker, but he talked rather more directly than you do, sir. According to his account, he was born in Jerusalem, given the name of Ahasuerus, was present at the crucifixion of Jesus, and since that time had travelled much, required little persuasion to talk of Christ and His history, to which he was the only living witness, and the confirmation of the Church's authority.'

'Ah!' the stranger responded excitedly. 'There you have it! The Church has encouraged belief in my existence in order that any stories they might attribute to me would corroborate their own; thus good Christians' attentions are distracted from the contradictions and confusions of the accounts of the Apostles. If I am an invention, sir, then I am, most certainly, a Christian lie.'

'That I can easily accept,' I replied after giving it a moment's thought. 'In my experience the Church's supporters are often mendacious in its interests. But what of the rest of the account as to this Ahasuerus taking part in the general cry of "Crucify him", calling for the deliverance of Barabas, and helping to bring about the sentence of death upon Jesus, after which they said the treacherous Jew hurried back to his workshop knowing that his innocent quarry must pass that way, and wishing to enjoy the scene? So that when the Son of God was led past, he spat upon him, cursed him, and bid him hurry. Whereupon Jesus looked sternly at him and replied thus: "I go to My Father, but thou shalt tarry till I return," or some

97

such words, the accounts varying in regard to Christ's actual response, it being beyond the capacity, apparently, of the most earnest of disciples to accurately recall even one single line of dialogue.'

He glanced at me sharply. 'From where did you', he enquired, 'get that precise line about tarrying?'

I explained to him that I had probably improved upon the so-called original quoted in the stodgy little German pamphlets; but that this was the sense of the curse. It would be taken to fulfil the prophecy in Apocalypse that 'some shall seeke death and shall not finde it'. Though why this bad-tempered cobbler should deserve such prophetic recognition was never clear to me.

'I have already explained,' the stranger replied, frowning, 'that my presence as a witness to the true events of that time has the Church's blessing.'

I answered him shortly, 'So I have understood you to say just now, sir, but perhaps you will be good enough to tell me what precisely you said to the alleged Messiah then.'

The fellow sighed profoundly. 'My dear sir, I fear that this will be difficult for you to believe, but the truth of the matter is that I, an early upholder of the kindly creed of Jesus and other young rabbis, merely suggested to Him that He hurry in order that He might not have the burden of bearing the cross-piece for His crucifixion longer than was necessary. My actual words were "Hurry along, Lord Jesus", after which it was my intention to whisper to Him that we, His ardent followers, had arranged an ambush and rescue a little farther along the road, and that He should rest there, thus enabling us, His supporters, to carry him off quickly down a narrow passage, in the floor of which there was a forgotten staircase to the endless caverns and ancient catacombs below the city.'

Much taken with this ingenious and credible account, I observed that this very sensible story had never before been heard. 'Was it not strange that Jesus did not recognize you as one of His own?' I enquired.

'He was hardly in a fit state to recognize anyone,' Ahasuerus explained, 'the Romans having vented their brutal disciplines upon His body, and the cross-piece being of old olive wood and very heavy. Though He was of the same age as myself, prayer and fasting had left Jesus in poor physical condition. Consequently when some brutish fellow jeered at Him, it took Him some moments before He was able to turn His head in that direction. When He eventually did so, He confused my kindly advice with the vicious sneers of my neighbour, an Edomite rug-seller. Whereupon the Christ fixed me with His slightly asymmetrical dark eyes and issued His well-known, but as you observe, invariably misquoted curse.'

'What, as a matter of scholarly interest, did He actually say?'

'To tell the simple truth, I was so stunned by the strange dark force that emanated from His eyes that I do not remember hearing it. Clearly, however, it had something to do with wandering about the world until what has since become popularly known as the Second Coming.'

I looked at the fellow with genuine admiration. 'You really are good at this,' I complimented him.

'Thank you,' he said. Supporting his own legend, he continued, 'After a millennium or so one does become quite good at being what everybody insists one is: immortally bad.'

'So,' I said, 'you maintain that you are in your present enviable situation as a result of mistaken identity, and that you have become the Wandering Jew by an error of judgement by an exhausted man, still strong enough in the sublime energy to lay upon your undeserving shoulders this burdensome task. Do I have you right now, sir?'

'You do,' he replied, nodding solemnly. 'Indeed I was at the time (and suppose I still am), a Greek. My name was Cartophilus –'

'"Much beloved"?' I translated. 'Certainly not, it seems, by your short-sighted leader.'

'I was a singularly beautiful child and could have found a comfortable life in any Greek temple had my father not needed my assistance in his workshop where I became adept in the art of making a style of sandal which I was interested to observe recently in Munich is coming back into fashion. My father had known the carpenter who was Jesus's father, and once bartered shoes for his entire family against an excellent set of chairs and a table, all of cedar wood. He carpentered only the finest merchandise. But to resume my melancholy story, every half-century I fall into a profound sleep, returning from which I am once again the age I was when I was condemned, so unfairly, to what for all ordinary purposes is life eternal.' The Greek (if I believed him) sighed profoundly and then yawned as if the endless repetitions of his life had left him irremediably tired.

'I take it,' I said, 'that your position is not entirely devoid of satisfactions. After all, a thirty-three-year-old Greek is more likely to succeed as a lover than an eighty-three-year-old itinerant Jewish maker of sandals in an unfashionable style.' He sighed again. I persisted anxiously, 'I take it that you are still able to practise and enjoy coitus?'

'I fear so,' he said. 'Just as my appetite for roast pork remains with me, so do all the other playful instincts of a healthy man. Oh, the tedium of having to spend yet another half-century indulging appetites which offer no variety whatsoever!'

'Come, come now, sir,' I shook my finger at him, deeply shocked. 'Here I am at seventy-two spending much of my time either remembering past conquests or plotting a final one before Death empties his much more reliable poison ring into my cup of sops, yet I cannot believe that I would tire of even a couple of millennia of such diversions, in spite of your silly magical demonstration. After all, one rises every morning, opens the window and breathes fresh air (a very mild intoxicant at best) with enormous pleasure. Why then should infinitely more intoxicating satisfactions please one less? Man's life is but repetition, and the only difference

101

between mine and yours is that mine has an unavoidable end. No, sir, I would gladly change places with you and let you inherit, with the greatest pleasure in the world, that final embrace which I do not look forward to with any eagerness whatsoever; while I wander the world being mistaken for a pariah Jew, renewing my vital juices every half-century or so and building up an amorous history which would render Casanova's score a miniscule achievement in erotic history.'

The young man looked at me with melancholy old eyes. 'Ah, sir,' he sighed, 'it is clear that you do not know what it is to be a Jew. Let me unwind for you an accounting which must appal any human heart. Let me list for you idiotic slanders and insane calumnies, absurd accusations and savage threats. I shall tell you of communities built upon the ashes of their forebears, raised with labour and love only to be burnt down again by mindless fire. I, Ahasuerus, kept upon this earth to witness the truths and blessings of Christ's gift to all mankind, am equally fit to account the crimes of His followers upon His people. Ah, sir, my tale is as endless and melancholy as my wanderings. Do not wish so extended and blighted a life upon yourself. Oh, I could tell you, sir –'

Concerned to divert the fellow from his miserable and pointless narration, I interrupted. 'But you say you are in truth no Jew, but a Greek,' I remarked. 'Why have you not asserted it and thus escaped an unearned fate as a member of the accursed race?'

'My poor sir,' he replied, 'how can I encourage you to understand that once one has been denominated a Jew, it is impossible to escape, for the more one protests to the contrary, the more the Gentiles assume one is lying, and the more of a Jew one ends up becoming. For while the Jews themselves maintain that he is a Jew who is born of a Jewish mother, it is equally true that he is a Jew whom the Gentiles insist is one.'

'But to the facts, sir,' I persisted, 'if you have spoken truth and are not indeed a lying Jew, then why should you accept the unbearable consequences of the mistaken curse of an exhausted and deranged self-styled Son of God?' While enjoying this game of my companion's, I was determined to force him to an admission that his fantastic assertions were the mere inventions of a travelling confidence man. 'Why,' I repeated, 'have you simply not wandered according to your own inclinations, discarding the antique costume you wear and substituting some less identifiable trade or profession for the traditional cobbler's equipment of the Wandering Jew? I could, I assure you, in spite of my reduced means and the limited years at my disposal, show you a disguise or two which would enable you to pass as a Gentile gentleman in any company.'

'Sir,' he responded doubtfully, 'you do not comprehend the power of the dark force which emanated from Him who cursed me. You must consider the power of an evil eye projected by the best Man in the world. In that moment all His great strength of good was concentrated upon blasting my atoms into an eternity of millennia. It is a complicated physical and chemical process which I am unable to explain, but it shall, I believe, in the fullness of time, come to be understood, and when it is, I fear all humanity will wander like the accursed Jew through unending shades.'

'Poetry and mysticism apart,' I said contemptuously, 'I do believe that you have made too much of your misfortune and that a more phlegmatic and ebullient temperament and a more optimistic attitude towards life would benefit you. Come, young man. You are talking with one who has experienced the worst as well as the best of life and has magnificently conquered both. Let me be your tutor. Let us consider your conundrum reasonably and sagaciously, and, I have no doubt that, by the time the coach that is to take us out of this dreary village arrives, your future will be as hopeful as my own was at your age.' I have no idea why I was permitting myself to cheer and encourage this young trickster. Perhaps it was the spectacle of his unalloyed misery which, simulated or not, appealed to my heart and flattered me into believing that my own situation was not nearly as bad as I had imagined it to be. Indeed how encouraging it is when one is in misery to witness the even greater misery of others! The young man dashed a tear from his eye. 'Come, sir,' I encouraged him, 'I have ever found that true manliness affronts misery. Tell yourself that this night the wanderings of the Jew shall cease for ever and that he will escape from this tedious prison as the ageing but dauntless Casanova has escaped from his.'

'But sir,' the young man anguished, 'what can I offer you in exchange for your admirable advice?'

And now we had come to the point. 'I recollect,' I advised him, 'from the several accounts I have read of the powers of the Wandering Jew, that he may part with a parcel of his own years whenever he wishes, adding them to the total of one more mortal than himself. If I cannot be young again, and indeed I have long suspected that this is the case, then let me persist in being old for as long as possible; for life always retains a faint trace of sweetness. Even warm polenta is pleasant mushed between toothless molars (provided of course that it is not piddled). I did tell you, I believe, of the quality of the food in the establishment of His Excellency of Duchkov? Never mind. To the point. I will trade you a new persona for a handful of years. Speak! How does such an exchange attract you?'

The young man studied me with some kind of amazement. 'But surely, Signor Casanova,' he said, 'it has already been demonstrated to you this night that magic is merely another human folly. Do you persist, you who have always vaunted your lack of belief in anything mystic, upon maintaining confidence in this coloured glass bauble? How would you know whether or not the years I award you were actual until it was too late?'

'Ah,' I said, 'I am now in the seventy-third year of my life, which is some two years longer than was projected for me by the great astrologer Count Alessandro di Cagliostro, who calculated much of my life to come some years ago in Paris. We spent an entire night in discussion during which he projected the end of the French monarchy in the latter years of this century. I submitted to him that if it were to happen so, the rebellion would be, in part, a revolt of men unable to bear any longer the monstrous domination of the fair sex who, in France, have ever held nefariously in their perfumed fingers all the affairs of Man. Once such a rebellion is mounted, I told him, its fire will run through the world, as rapidly as did the other French contagion, the pox, and men will wreak a dreadful revenge upon women for our years of enslavement by enfranchising them, whereupon they would lose their power over us. Look to your manners, ladies, I said, for the end of your time of dominion is at hand. I personally have always enjoyed being enslaved to the fair sex, although I do not believe it has been good for my moral character. But I am a little tired and wandering from the point, which is that my allotted span, the good man's Biblical three-score-and-ten, is some two years over its limit, and, feeling as I do on a good day no more than fifty-five, and looking, in a good light after a careful *toilette*, no more than fifty, I am inclined to think that the wise Count was possibly misguided in his deductions and that I may enjoy another decade or so. In any case, although I have never been more than ordinarily superstitious (all we Venetians are a little, you know), I see no possible harm in putting together the best auspices and omens available. If the Wandering Jew exists and you are he, and he has the power to bestow even a few years, then what possible harm can it do for them to be endowed in me?'

'Signor Casanova,' the young man replied, 'I have enjoyed your company through this night which, twice each century, is a melancholy time of enforced renewal for me. Your youthful enthusiasm for life and charming greed for its dubious diets has eased my unwilling transition, and though I look forward with loathing to the fifty years I inherit tonight, I do not hold the ineffectualness of your poisonous potion against you, just as you, I hope, do not blame me for the limited effectiveness of my magic. Why can we not settle for the imperfectibility of our lives as Destiny has constructed them, going about our businesses without complaint? Surely it is better for us to remember a night spent in pleasant conversation than to add further unsatisfactory experiments to the avoidance of the inevitable?'

'Come, sir,' I replied, 'respect my experience in such encounters. I understand well enough that you are an ingenious trickster and that there is no profit for anyone other than yourself in treating with you; but I myself have tricked my way beyond my allotted span and have a certain respect for anyone of our trade who can hold my attention for as long as you have this night. I, who taught Cagliostro gematria and the subtleties of numerology with my own little Kabbalah based upon the

107

divine *Orlando Furioso*, a simple trick which, incidentally, was the means whereby I won the wealthiest and most beautiful girl in the Netherlands for my betrothed, although I have always been too firmly wed to freedom to undertake any other marriage – ah, yes, Marietta was her name, the beautiful and genuinely virgin daughter of sixteen years of a father, a wealthy Amsterdam merchant much taken with me for my courtly style and manners, who prevailed upon me to court his child which, since I had plans for his wealth, I was gracious enough to undertake. This Marietta, the only enchanting creature I have ever known with a passion for arithmetic, found my numerology quite fascinating. In that year of 1737 or 8, I believe it was, yes, 1738 it was for sure, I showed her how to make the pyramid with the proper numbers and other silly ceremonies, uncovering a revelation which amazed her. This enchanting child, I must explain, possessed a dimple on her chin in the midst of which there was a little dark mole garnished with three or four extremely fine hairs. Now these punctuation points to love I have often observed are duplicated on corresponding points of the body. I therefore concluded that the divine little Marietta had a similar mole in a certain place a virtuous Dutch girl does not exhibit even to gentlemen with excellent bankers' references. So I made her my pyramid and extracted from it the advice that at the entrance of her temple of love the dear creature had a mole precisely like that which appeared upon her chin.'

The young man seemed quite fascinated by my story. 'And did she, did she indeed?' he encouraged me.

'Indeed she did,' I replied, 'conclusively proving my theory of the disposition of moles on the female body, an account of which I have included in my Memoirs.' Suddenly I remembered a less pleasant vision. 'It is a miserable trick of the memory in age that it hops like a flea from a fair body to a foul one. In the Leads of Venice, from which I am the only one ever to have escaped, there was a contemptible friar whose face was decorated with a dozen or so black hairy moles. I do not care to think where else they populated his obnoxious body. Tell me, dear boy, where was I?'

'We were talking of tricks,' he reminded me, 'and I had expressed my doubt that you had anything to gain from any of mine. Would it not be better, Signor, since you seem a little tired, for us to sleep the hour or so before dawn so as to commence the next stage of our journey refreshed?'

I emptied the remains of the brandy down my throat and felt an immediate surge of energy. 'Teach me this trick which you are so eager not to communicate. As I remember, and I have always had a faultless memory for such things, the pamphlets all agree that the great charge of energy which permeated you from the baleful eyes of Our Lord, which energy has sustained you through subsequent centuries, this immortal force is supposed to irradiate from your own eyes, bearing a shadow of that power which had carried you through the years. Such is the legend, and its claims do not seem unreasonable.'

'But my dear sir,' the young fellow protested, 'you are surely not so gullible as to believe these silly figments of the folklore of ignorant people? I swear I do not wish to take advantage of you. Why are you insisting that I do?'

'I will not be refused!' I exclaimed, the brandy and fatigue striving against one another in my breast. 'If the trick is a good one, then, who knows, it may serve me well in my next confrontation with some noble Teutonic ordure. I am running out, sir; I cannot afford to pass a good trick.'

The now young man (and I had to admit that his youth seemed as entirely authentic as had his age previously. Could there be truth in all this magical nonsense of which I had so often made a profitable business? In God's world all is possible!), this young man looked at me with ancient eyes. 'But have you not yourself often observed, sir,' he said, 'that in all attempts to get the better of Fortune one is well-served by a happy stroke of calculation and by a dexterity quite independent of luck? In a word,' he continued, 'have you not observed the principle of cheating intelligently whenever the odds required it?'

I appreciated the fellow's serious consideration of my career and reputation. 'Certainly I believe,' I opined learnedly, 'that one may improve one's chances so long as one does not do it in too crude a manner, for it is most damaging to one's credit to be caught out in such manoeuvres. One should not scruple to cheat (if one can) empty-headed people, scoundrels, fools and women, though as to the latter, the inevitable mutual deceptions of love may be considered a matter of give and take. Of any two lovers, one or the other must needs be the dupe. But as to other fools, they are insolent and presumptuous, and to take them in is to glorify one's intelligence; I hate all fools and feel myself degraded in their company. But let us get back to our business, sir.'

Still my companion delayed. 'Are we not all of us,' he asked, 'a little foolish sometimes, and should we not therefore show some charity towards the gullible?'

'You may do as you like,' I advised him, 'but I, sir, shall reserve my right to never give a fool the smallest charitable consideration. And now let me ask you, once and for all, can you or can you not oblige me in the matter of a magical experience? If not, say so, and I will still refer to you in my Memoirs, for you are as good a trickster as I have met with in a life full of memorable jaunts with distinguished members of the Mercurial academy.'

The young man studied me with sad eyes full of compassion. 'Oh, sir,' he sighed, 'what great credit you have brought to your ill-treated and much-misunderstood brotherhood! I can, if you insist, give you a taste of my game. Afterwards, you may decide for yourself whether you wish to continue playing it. Are you ready, sir?'

'Proceed!' I instructed him eagerly.

'Keep your eyes upon my ring,' he advised me, flashing before me a ring with a strangely bright gem in it which I had not (most unlike me) hitherto observed. 'Concentrate upon the light,' he said, and I did. He counted backwards from one hundred, and I felt myself pass over into a new and unpleasantly alien world. As he did so, I murmured, 'But you surely drank the poison, did you not?'

'Not necessarily,' he answered, but as he continued his explanation, I lost him.

(V)

*It gave me no pleasure to know
that this journey was likely to go
on for ever*

ALTHOUGH MY FEET were as hard as iron, thick as the epidermis of an elephant, and shod in good heavy sandals of my own making, they were bruised by the endless stony road which I walked, clad in an ancient caftan and bearing a heavy bag upon my back. It gave me no pleasure to know that this journey was likely to go on for ever, for I constantly reviewed in my mind conditions with which my companion of the night, Jew-like, had forgotten to acquaint me. The most damaging of these arrangements was that I could not spend more than twenty-four hours in any place. This made anything but the most superficial intercourse with others impossible, for since most of my walking was done by day, and the majority of people are not interesting night-companions, I often found myself in lonely circumstances. Of course you may say that a night is all the time traditionally necessary to Casanova, the great lover, to assert his erotic vocation. Thank you for your lecherous thoughts, but I must confess that, even for me, a millennium or so of lubricity had been enough. I had as little serious interest left in women as had my old friend the chief eunuch in Constantinople. Yes, a little diddling here and there, but what of that?

My itinerary, set by some Divine force, took me

115

through only the most miserable of human habitations and placed me in the most uncomfortable of lodgings. Fortunately, however, the controlling power over my endless peregrination did not require me to have much contact with Jews, although passing through countless small towns and villages of middle Europe, I inevitably encountered them as, like ants, they busily rebuilt their lives and livelihoods recently ruined for no good reason other than pious Chrsitian idiocy. To the idiots themselves I had an unpleasant and uncomfortable compulsion to reveal myself, usually in churches, at the height of the service, as witness of Christ's mercy. As they yawned and sang off-key and groped one another or picked their noses, I would stand up, disturbing their innocent Sunday devotions by announcing my mission. I tried time and again to break myself of this uncivilized and embarrassing habit, but it was yet another of the unmentioned conditions of my useless immortality, for I had not realized that I was to be a kind of travelling salesman for the dubious salves and potions which spring from the Rock of Peter.

Local pastors were much excited by me, many of them subsequently writing bad pamphlets about my appearance in their localities. They happily noted the melancholy of my demeanour, the oracular quality of my voice, and the totally calculable message I bore; but they were poor company, their viands miserable, and their wine sour, if sacramental. Good Christian I had been all my life (or at least indifferently bad, but well-raised in the mysteries of the Church, having received my instruction at the cushioned feet of Popes), but I was nevertheless appalled to find that immortality consisted of endless simplistic theological discussions with half-educated imbeciles perfectly suited to their congregations.

In despair, I occasionally threw myself upon the hospitality of the Jews, clustered together like field-mice in winter in miserable small crowded townships. They mistakenly took me for one of themselves, largely because my costume and the depredations of life among the Gentiles had given me that pinched and persecuted look. Naturally I did not bother to enlighten them, for I remembered from my former happy life as a mortal libertine that they did occasionally secrete in their hovels delicious pâtés and nubile daughters. But Hell hath no punishment to award greater than the delicate digestion my endless travelling now induced in me, I who could always digest anything piquant enough to pass the entrance of my well-forged teeth! And as to the seduction of their innocent Rachels and Rebeccas, I swear I had nothing more threatening under my caftan than a patrol of hungry fleas. These may have mingled with those of the occasionally pretty quarries my nights in Jewry presented, but, if they did so, it was not to provide me with rich meals or delicate satisfactions. And yet again, endless theological discussions, for theology is the second business of the Jews who engage in it with as much energy and expertise as they apply to making money.

Such discussions (which explode the mind of Man) result from the Jewish postulate that there is a God of Law over-ruling a notoriously non-law-abiding human species which must be punished for its sins of omission and commission to the end of time; which blessed relief, they assert, will be heralded by the arrival of a Messiah who will lead righteous humanity, led by righteous Jewry, into an eternal Paradise. In the correspondingly inane Christian discussions, everyone (especially the Jews) is being punished by an endlessly loving God who hates having to behave so unpleasantly and only does so because Christ (His Son) is not yet wholly accepted and His teachings not entirely in successful practice among Men. But no great success is anticipated by even the most enthusiastic Christian dogmatists, since it is written in Revelations that only a hundred thousand or so of the enraptured Christian righteous will enter Paradise. In spite of the depressing fact that their number (even after systematic persecutions) substantially exceeds this figure, the conversion or utter eradication of the Jews, the originators and distributors of the Christ cult among the pagans (all Christian peoples were formerly pagan), becomes a prime mission. Once achieved, this dubious victory will herald the return of Christ, that short-sighted Messiah who, according to my information, blasted a harmless Gentile into being a Wandering Jew. But here I am myself engaging in the absurdities and contradictions of theology! The habit must have infected me during those endless pointless discussions which I witnessed in such utter boredom, concluding only that the task of relating an endlessly good God to a consistently bad world requires more than a little intellectual chicanery.

Occasionally these Jewish discussions were interrupted by drunken Chrsitians who, observing their high and Holy festivals, arrived with clubs searching out a brutal release for their sudden attack of piety. They would beat the Jews, murder the most harmless, and rape both pretty and ugly girls (some of whose fleas had cavorted with mine), quite indiscriminately. They would then burn everything and, in the small hours of the morning, stumble homewards with headaches but warm inside, knowing they had vindicated and revenged Our Lord for His crucifixion by these very same dastardly Jews. As soon as the last peasant had left, the Jews would begin rebuilding their lives with what many thought remarkable courage, but which I, for my part, considered an absurd waste of energy. For both they and their Gentile persecutors knew that their communities, once again wealthy, would be over-taxed and drained of every last hidden ducat by the aristocracy, and then tossed to a peasantry infuriated by its own endless enslavement to those who paid for their gambling and whoring with the sweat of the peasants and the fruits of Jewish industry. So, like tortured bulls, they fell upon the impoverished Jews scrambling for a living between theological discussions, and, after yet another orgy of rape, pillage, and murder (to the glory of God), returned to slave for their illiterate and brutal good Christian overlords.

Why did they all bother? The pretensions of the victims and the fury of the persecutors seemed alike ridiculous to a rational man. I saw the Inquisition doing its fine work testing the pretences of these miserable people to having been chosen for anything other than the merciless sport of Gentiles, and, from time to time, witnessed mass-conversions. But generally speaking, this stubborn people, even when not wholly delighted with their chosen way of life, refused to accept a better one. For they truly believed that their mysterious and terrible God had chosen them for some obscure purpose, quite apart from providing profitable pastime and industry for Christians. Their unending theological discussions were investigations into this obscure divine objective, and, to discover what it was, they juggled with the conundrums of Kabbalah and tottered through endless mazes of Talmudical wisdom between celebrating obscure rituals to flatter and glorify their indescribable and indecipherable God.

So the years passed into centuries, but the bloody game continued, and still I witnessed it, walking on my painful feet, repairing shoes and testifying oracularly in churches and in ghettos to the perfection of Christ's plan for the salvation of mankind. It was tedious work, without much intellectual satisfaction, yet it caused me to ponder profoundly whether or not there was some meaning to this area of our generally disgusting human history. And then, one day, as I rested in a quiet Jewish village recently pillaged and burned by the pious, the revelation came to me. No birds sang among the ashes, and the deathly silence was relieved only by the mewing of a litter of catlings born during the sacred celebrations; yet there, in the desolation, it came to me that this unspeakable agony chosen for the Jews was, in fact, the only immortality available in our human history. I, the Wandering Gentile, now testified that no humanly understandable or enjoyable benefit was discoverable in such immortality. Man, Jew, Gentile, eternal traveller, all were equally cursed by it. And so, at last, I came to hate all that was not simply mortal and I longed again to be an old man with a sensible and hopefully decent human death ahead of me.

Yet disgusted and exhausted as I was by this endless exposure to theology, so persistent is my invention and *esprit* that I found myself, for want of other intellectual victuals, chewing upon the cosmogonic problems presented and, inevitably, I produced my own original theory. First I considered the so-called heresy of the Manicheans who maintained that the world is the domain of the Devil, true Lord of the Earth and of Man; it is a delusion which has justified much crudely evil behaviour. But look about the world and observe its beauty and harmony; can one convincingly dismiss all that as a Satanic delusion, maintaining that only the dark and devilish aspects of life are a true reflection of its dominant evil spirit? I think not. There is far too much work of a supremely good

121

artist in the world, it seems to me, for it to be wholly dismissed as a delusion of Satan. On the other hand, supposing we conclude that the world is indeed God's domain, and so account for its light and beauty, then we are left with a thorny question to answer. Could the Author of such harmonious creation also be responsible for the one animal species which constantly wrecks Divine Harmony? Surely, observing Man and his endless abominations, a logical mind might reasonably conclude that Humanity is the Devil's plaything, and that at the great feast of life a kingly God has thrown mankind, an unconsidered tidbit, to His dogs, to gnaw and play with at their pleasure.

Of course, I realized while projecting this naïve Casanovan cosmogony, that I was perpetrating as great an absurdity as the theologians whose discussions had given me so many headaches. Indeed, I remained convinced, as I always have been, that all there is to the entire debate is that Man, feeling good, projects his emotions beyond himself and calls them God, but when feeling bad, denominates his long dark shadow a Satanic Force. It is interior matter exteriorized, and that is all. But it amused me to play this hoary intellectual game, and, eventually, it seemed to me that I could, without too much trouble, establish a new religion. I would maintain, in simple, that the world is God's, but that Man belongs to the Devil. I would be the High Priest of this newly-founded deistic diabolism, and eager converts would heap their worldly possessions before me in exchange for

122

wise sayings and blessings. Thinking of the practical possibilities of my cosmogonic discovery, I was eager to return to being Casanova. There is still a trick or two left in the old fool, I assured myself. I have not been dubbed the Venetian Mercurius for nothing. And yes, I must not forget my new medicine for the bowels, for surely a man equipped with a new religion and a good laxative may aspire to great heights, in spite of his age. And so I protested as loudly as I could against the endlessly wearying affliction of interminable life. 'Let me go back!' I called. 'Let me return!' I demanded. 'Casanova is a man!' I cried out in that empty blackened ruin. 'Let it be enough! To the Devil or God with all supra-human pretensions and preoccupations! Let us live and die meaninglessly like mere men, and let all gods and demons mind their own infernal businesses and keep their noses out of ours! Mind your own business!' I cried out furiously, again and again. 'Life is meaningless; but more than enough!'

'Signor Casanova! Awake, awake, sir!' Stichka's loud coarse voice and bad breath suddenly assaulted me, and I awoke, stiff and cold. The fire was long dead, and so was my arm on which I had been lying on the bench where I had earlier discovered my night's companion apparently dead and then suspiciously rejuvenated. As the candle-end guttered out in a pool of evil-smelling mutton fat, and the first light of morning struck through the shuttered window dimly illuminating the ghastly corpse of a half-consumed pig upon the

table, I peered about me looking after the wild magician. 'What are you doing in those clothes, Signor? I took you for the damned Jew. What a blessing I did not punch you in the ear as was my intention! Where is the devil? Hurry, sir, the carriage will be here any minute,' Stichka wheezed and fumed, and it did not take me long to realize that whilst I had slept the disturbed sleep induced by my missing companion, he had taken advantage of my helplessness and stolen my clothes, and, on further investigation, the few miserable possessions I had brought with me from the castle. Yet I was greatly relieved to realize what had taken place, for I would much sooner be humanly tricked by a clever travelling confidence man than have to account for my nocturnal experiences as a supernatural encounter with a phantom. I infinitely preferred to write off the whole affair as just another bad night of bad drink, bad companions, and bad dreams.

'The swine has left only his tools!' Stichka exclaimed. 'And where are your honour's bags? Blast his vitals, the old bugger has stolen the very clothes off your back! What is it, sir? Do you not comprehend what has happened to you?'

'Come, come, Stichka,' I comforted the irate innkeeper, 'make me some coffee and let us consider the situation reasonably and sensibly.'

Mumbling and grumbling, Stichka ordered his scullions, who now appeared rubbing their eyes with dirty fists, to remake the fire and put water on to boil. 'Hang these Jews, the lot of them!' he muttered. 'As soon as one appears, we should string him up. It's the only way to defend ourselves from the brood of Satan. But how', he addressed himself to me, 'did he get you out of your clothes and into his own? I know you gentlemen get up to some strange games, but isn't adopting an old Jew's fleas going a bit far in the pursuit of curious pleasures?'

'My dear Stichka,' I replied, 'an excess of your appalling brandy has made the events of the night quite obscure to me. Nevertheless, it is clear that I have been tricked and robbed, but the loss is mine and I would be grateful if you would permit me to do my own wailing over it. I have lost a fine pocket-watch, the gift of a noble lady, not to mention a purse containing all my funds and a number of other considerable trifles.'

As I considered the sentimental items of which the cunning trickster had relieved me, the satisfaction I felt in the perfect normality of being robbed, rapidly drained away. How, I reveried, could I, who, in more than half-a-century, had practised successfully all the tricks devised by the subtlety of Man, how, other than by true witchcraft, could I have changed my familiar role for that of victim? I recollected another most miserable time of my life, a time when all my schemes and hopes had collapsed, and I was desperately induced to take work in Venice for the Inquisitors of State. So I had travelled back to the city of stagnant canals in a dirty carriage with dirty companions. As I nibbled then on a dry chicken's leg, I was full of dark thoughts and forebodings, for though I was only in my still-vigorous fifties, the world I had known and conquered was decaying fast. The gallant life of a courtly adventurer was rapidly becoming an anachronism. Wherever I appeared I was treated as a grand old story which had become, through endless unsubtle telling, a bit of a joke. As I was borne then, itching and cold, to Venice, I was unable to believe that Jacques Casanova, the world's envy, free of all burdens except his own instincts, I, the Chevalier of Total Licence, was returning of my free will to the contemptible life of a state-spy, a watcher over the morals (forsooth!) of my fellow-citizens! I, the lover of adventurers, gypsies, actors and courtesans, the friend of singers, artists and musicians, the brother of vagabonds, all enlisted under the banner of Mercury and blessed by the great Goddess of Situations as we pursued our pleasures undeterred by the strictures of those grey

126

ones who consider that the greatest virtue lies in resisting the strongest inclinations, so was I, the King of Free Souls, become the slave of dull devils with apoplectic faces.

Ah, Freedom! I apostrophized, we artists, motley travelling clowns, wander in thy paths, picking thy delicate flowers, gobbling up thy delicious truffles, and, though we frequently slip upon the cow-pats which nourish both, shall we languish in the end in the repellent prisons of respectability? Is this our gallant life's last pitiful stand? Oh, with what disgust did I then ponder (as I do now) the crowning irony, that I, who have flouted the morality of every state in Europe, should betray my life's earlier proud work with the detested custodianship of the moral imbecilities of the tyrants of a petty Republic! Stichka's ugly serving-maid now brought me fresh coffee, and as I sniffed its aroma and sipped it, like Paul upon the road to Tarsus, I surveyed the events of my life yet again, searching for an epiphany, or at least the slightest hint of what I should do next.

Item. I remembered my mother, a bad actress, produced me at Venice on 2nd April, Easter Day, of the year 1725. She had, the night before, a strong desire for crawfish. I am very fond of all creatures of the sea, but what of that?

Item. At baptism, I was named Jacques-Jerome. I was an idiot until I was eight-and-a-half years old. Then I was cured by magic and brilliantly applied myself to study. At the age of sixteen I was made a doctor and given the habit of a priest so that I might

127

go seek my fortune at Rome where the daughter of my French instructor was the cause of my being dismissed by my patron, Cardinal Aquaviva. Already I was sworn brother, it seemed, to catastrophe.

Item. At eighteen, I entered the military service of my country, and went to Constantinople, but after two colourfully unprofitable years, I returned to Venice where I perversely embraced the wretched and rascally life of a violinist in a pit-orchestra which horrified all my distinguished friends, and myself!

Item. At twenty-one, a high noble of Venice adopted me as his son, and, having thus become rich, I went to Italy, France, Germany, and Vienna where I was intimate with many great men and women. Returning to Venice, a famous gallant, I was entrapped by the State Inquisitors who imprisoned me in the Leads, from which no one had ever escaped; but I did after fifteen months, and fled to Paris.

My affairs prospered, and I became a millionaire through my management of the State lottery. I would have made a second fortune from manufacturing copies of rich tapestries which became all the rage, but my workers were all girls, who so distracted me from business affairs that, once again, I became bankrupt.

I made money again in Holland; suffered misfortune in Stuttgart; was received with honours in Switzerland; visited that ass Voltaire; adventured in Genoa, Marseilles, Florence and Rome, where Pope Rezzonico made me a Chevalier of Saint Jean-Latran and an apostolic protonotary. This was in 1760, in which same year I enjoyed good fortune at the tables in Naples; carried off a nun in Florence; and, stupidly, went to England, which was a great misfortune for it is a cold and repellent puritan country. I soon deserted it, narrowly avoiding the clumsy gibbet which the coarse English favour for those who ridicule them.

Afterwards I searched (but in vain) for my Lady Fortune in Berlin and Petersburg; glimpsed her in Warsaw; but there lost all through a pistol duel with General Branicki, who idiotically thought me a lover of men and whose abdomen my bullet pierced. It would have been less fatal to have put a hole in his head, the dumb ox. So I was obliged to leave Poland, returning to Paris where a *lettre de cachet* promptly obliged me to leave. I went to Spain where I met with even greater misfortunes,

129

through making nocturnal visits to the mistress of the *Vice-roi*, who was a great and impertinent scoundrel, but excellent with the rapier.

After spitting blood for eighteen months, I shamefully sought the Venetians' favour by publishing a Defence of their disgusting tyrannical government in three ponderous volumes (may I be forgiven!). In 1770 the English Minister at the Court of Turin sent me, well-recommended, to Leghorn; whence I repaired to Rome where a happy love-affair caused me to follow a noble lady to Naples. There, three months later, another love-affair caused me to return rapidly to Rome after I had measured swords (for the third time) with the notorious duellist, Count Medini, poor fellow, who died four years ago in detested London in debtors' prison.

So many of us fine duellists are dead, though I myself feel well enough after a singularly bad night. I remember suddenly the Archduke Leopold (he too is dead), who ordered me to leave his dominions within three days; I had there a mistress who, by my advice, became a Duchess in Bologna. After all that and too much more, I was weary, weary of running about Europe, and, exhausted, I cravenly solicited the mercy of the Venetian State Inquisitors to permit me to go back. Two years later in Trieste the black-hearted swine graciously granted me permission. Surprisingly, my return to the stinking lovely city, after nineteen years, was one of the most pleasant moments of my life, in spite of the shame of my new occupation. Spying protected me for several years, till again I became embroiled with the pernicious Venetian State and quickly vacated my ungrateful country for Paris where my brother, the rich painter, lives, but he would never help me in spite of all he owes me. Yet I forgive the wretch. No, I do not. Damn his soul to Hell!

Where was I? Oh, yes, my friend M. Foscarini, the Venetian Ambassador, an ignoramus for whom I wrote most elegant dispatches, died in my arms, killed by the gout which had mounted into his chest, and so I must travel again, like a veritable Wandering non-Jew, to Berlin, where I hoped the Academy would offer me a position; but *en route* my friend, the Prince de Ligne, introduced me to Count Waldstein at Teplitz, which led to my long imprisonment as librarian in Dux where, dreaming of freedom and my thousand ageing mistresses, I wrote my incomplete Memoirs. And now I sit here sipping bad coffee gently and wondering is this the end of the matter?

Much fussing and noise, neighing of horses, creaking of leather, Stichka rousing his demons, passengers stretching themselves before mounting the carriage. 'The carriage for Prague is here, Signor!' Stichka shouted at me. 'Hurry, Signor Casanova! By order of our great Graf of Waldstein the chaise waits for no man! Hurry, sir!' He rushed back to his business. I sighed again and chewed on a speck of bitter coffee and pondered why I, who never wished harm to any, except when they came between me and my elemental satisfactions, why

131

should I have been brought to such a pass? Have I not ever been eminently human? Have not my cravings for youth and immortality been entirely mortal? Am I not a man of the purest pattern? As I bite on the cold coffee grounds bitter in my mouth, I hear the carriage without. Stichka and his minions hurry in again and pester me like insane wasps, to hurry, hurry! But to what end should I hurry? Where is there left for me to go? What end is there to the journey, other than the only certainty in all men's lives? Oh, I am too human, too honest! Faintness overwhelms me. Perhaps I am, indeed, near to death. Well, and if so, my conscience is clear, for I know that I have been, withal, bad enough, which is as good as any true man ever is. I feel no pain, but a pleasurable weakness. I believe my end will be very quiet, gentle as the touch of a perfumed ghost, for my heart has always been true and my soul is relatively unspotted. Farewell to books and lovers all; *adieu mes rêves*, goodbye all you ghostly dreams out there, Casanova wishes you well in your adventures. Stichka! Where is the abominable Stichka? Will no one notice that I am dying? I hear the carriage passing on, the horses snorting, the harness creaking, the voices fading.

But no, I will not pass away in this pigsty looking like an itinerant Semite. I am an old gallant, and if I must die, I shall do so gallantly. I must hurry back to the castle of disgust. I have in my cedar chest there a barely-used silk court-dress. That red-cheeked minx will arrive at seven bringing persecution and polenta for breakfast. She shall see a

brilliant, distinguished and courtly Casanova, who, though he has returned to his hole like a mouse, still has the heart of a lion and the appearance of a dandy. So, up and away, Casanova! Lift your gouty body, raise your sinewy legs, *en avant*! Ah, Stichka, help me!

That little Bohemian slut with her big round blue eyes and her delicious little red apple cheeks, scrubbed up and properly dressed or undressed, might with a little training, pass for a lady, if she could be prevailed upon not to open her mouth, except in the way of duty, of course. I shall show her my last three little filthy Aretin drawings. How glad I am not to have sold all my educational material!

'Oh, Chevalier! Whatever is that naughty lady doing?'

'Saluting life, my dear – saluting life!'

I shall certainly improve upon our last little

episode. She may lie to the dirty groom or to His Excellency's contemptible Fauchenkircher, but Casanova knows well enough when he punctures a hymen, so do not dally with me, child! I am the Knight of the Golden Spur, mademoiselle! Ah, the clatter of her clumsy footsteps! Ah, my last mistress comes! Hurry to me, fortunate minx!

'Gnadig herr! Gnadig herr!' Nasty German trips prettily between her ripe lips. I shall teach her my secret thrust. *En garde*, queen of the morning!

"You vill be goot homme if I am komm?" I must teach the poor child French, meanwhile . . .

'Komm, komm to your god, my baby goddess!' Come and join my earliest lovely love Bettina; become sweet sister to ill-fated Lucy of Paséan; chatter with Christina, another simple peasant girl; be educated by intelligent Esther Hope, daughter of the wealthy Cologne banker, who inspired me to an entirely honourable courtship; learn tricks from the sagacious Marcolina; simulate the dreamy eyes of Clementina, my little blue-stocking; you will be attacked by a fair Amazon lady to whom I played butler in Zurich; Lady Pauline will corrupt you; the astute Madame Cornelys, mother of my lovely daughter, will show you how to become a great hostess; learn revenge from a little Spanish Countess; and, who knows, perhaps in time you will emulate the sweet and complete Henriette, the darling French spy who was, perhaps, the only woman for whom I ever truly cared. And if you cannot improve yourself through these lovely ladies, well then, I do not give up hope, for there

134

are a thousand others whose ghosts will smile upon us as we salute them with the ancient postures of love.

I shall take my stand away from the window where the morning light is unfriendly to me.

'Komm, komm, schöne Fraulein! I am ready for my end, little princess! Come quickly, take my life!' Ah, the grubby little angel!

Damn my soul, but I must hurry back before the rusty old sword crumbles to dust. Pray there is time to change into my other silk court-dress which is barely used and is, I am certain, in my cedar chest. I must remake my *maquillage* and put on my best wig. The court-dress is the one I wore when, in Holland, I was made, by the common request of the assembled nobility, Chevalier of Seingalt. Remember who you are, Casanova! Let that damned cackling Fauchenkircher (name like the broken crowing of an ancient cock) know that you are a famous philosopher, a superior mind, and above all, a true gentleman. He will crumble like the burst pages of a discarded manuscript. And I will finish mine, my Memoirs shall triumph over death. My fame in life will be excelled by my renown in the afterlife. And when I read my perorations to my dear old friend the Prince de Ligne and his chuckling nephew the Count von Waldstein and their noble friends of doubtful intelligence, they will smile while the tears flow from their eyes, and, as I reach my magnificent end, they will applaud and applaud and still applaud.

'The carriage waited as long as possible, sir.'

Stichka is very concerned and looks at me askance. 'What will you do now?'

'I care not if the carriage proceeds without me, Stichka, for, wherever it is going, I have already been there. Help me back to the loathsome *schloss* of Duchkov, my man. I feel a little weak.'

'Well, you drank three bottles of brandy through the night, your honour.'

'It was, Stichka, a remarkably long night.'

Giacomo Giralamo Casanova de Seingalt lived on, writing and complaining, until 4th June, 1798, when he yielded to a fatal bladder complaint. He was buried in the churchyard of Saint Barbara at Dux where the exact location of his grave is unknown. A tablet on the outside wall of the church tastefully celebrates his dates under an angelic image whose example he was never much inclined to follow. He never completed his Memoirs.